MARIE-HÉLÈNE LEBEAULT
AUTHOR OF THE EVERS SERIES

BLOOD
LEGACY

BLOOD MAGICK BOOK 3

First published by Beaches and Trails Publishing 2022
Copyright © 2022 by Marie-Hélène Lebeault

Legal deposit - Bibliothèque et Archives nationales du Québec, 2022
Legal deposit - Bibliothèque et Archives Canada, 2022

First edition
ISBN Paperback: 978-1-990656-44-6

Editing by Rachael Lammie
Cover art by MiblArt

ABOUT THE AUTHOR

Positive, uplifting books and stories.

Marie-Helene Lebeault lives in Quebec, Canada and is the mother of two young adults. A retired teacher, she now spends her days writing, translating academic manuals, and lending her voice to corporate training videos. She enjoys reading, hiking, and going to the beach. She is also an avid rollercoaster fiend and is on a mission to visit all the Six Flags amusement parks with her daughter. Every year, she travels for three weeks on a solo adventure to a new part of the world.

Follow on Social Media, she'd love to hear from you!

Website Email Newsletter

ALSO BY THE AUTHOR

The Evers Series

The Ancestors' Key

The Academy

The Time Walker

The World Jumper

The Complete Evers Series Box Set

The Blood Magick Trilogy

The Blood Mage

Blood Magick

Blood Legacy

Standalones

Clarity Castle

Anthologies

What Happens Next?: Readers Decide Which Story Becomes A Book

Novellas

Stranded with a Shifter: A YA Holiday Romance

Picture Books

Fairy Grandmother: Millie Goes to Antarctica

Fairy Grandmother: Millie Goes to the North Pole

Fairy Grandmother: Millie Goes to China

(Available in English, French, Spanish, German, and Italian)

This book is dedicated to my son whose insight was invaluable when I'd written myself into a corner.

ACKNOWLEDGEMENTS

I'd like to thank my editor, Rachael Lammie, for editing my daily pages every night so I could address the edits when I woke up in the morning while I was away on a writer's retreat. It made the book come together that much faster.

On that note, I'd also like to thank Janie and Gerard from *Go and Write* for organizing the retreat at the beautiful Kingsbrae International Residency for the Arts in beautiful St. Andrews by-the-Sea, New Brunswick. It was my first writer's retreat, but certainly not my last.

PROLOGUE

VARDO, Finnmark, 1663

"How do we keep the Witches from casting evil spells on us and the townsfolk while they're on the pyre, waiting to burn," whispered one of the guards, eyeing the eighteen women down in the Witches' hole.

"The King has suggested bloodletting. Enough to make them weak, but not enough to take their lives. These hags must suffer the consequences of aligning themselves with the devil," replied Brön, one of the King's physicians.

"What's to prevent them from cursing the one who's doing the bloodletting?" the guard continued.

"For one thing, we'll do it while they're asleep. For another, they'll all be bled at the same time," replied the man as patiently as he could. He disliked common folk and resented being sent on such distasteful errands.

"Won't they wake from the wounds, though?" asked the guard. He was a curious one. Brön had to give him that. He sighed. "Not if they drink the draft that we'll put in their daily water ration."

The guard's eyes grew large, and he tapped his nose as he winked. "You're a clever one, Sire."

Brön did not reply. He waited for the bucket to be brought over to him. When it arrived, he poured the sleeping draft inside and stirred it in with a wooden spoon. Gingerly, the guard took the bucket, attached it to the rope, and lowered it into the hole.

"I'll be back in an hour," said Brön.

THE DRAFT HAD PUT the Witches to sleep. It had been a good plan. Even if they could have tasted or smelled it in the water, it was the only water they received. Thus, the plan was a success. Eyeing the wooden trenches as they worked, the guard quizzed Brön some more. "They're for collecting the blood," Brön hastened.

"But why?" asked the guard as he went about cutting a Witch's wrist over the trencher while counting the way Brön had instructed; counting to ensure enough blood was let out to weaken the Witches.

"If we let the blood seep into the ground, it may leech into the river and contaminate the village," Brön explained. "Stop asking questions and focus on your counting. We don't want them to die, remember?"

"Aye, Sire," replied the guard gruffly.

It was a thankless task. The hole smelled like sweat, urine, and feces. Brön hated touching the vile, unwashed bodies of the unholy creatures. They could only carry a single torch, laden as they were, with the trenches and the bucket. Each trencher was poured into the bucket and wiped off with a rag.

When the task was done, they left the sleeping Witches. Upon waking, they'd see the rags tied around their wrists and feel the cuts on their skin. They would, however, be too weak to put up much of a fight as they were led to the pyre and to their eternal damnation.

FREDERIKSBORG CASTLE, Denmark, 1663

Niels, the King's head physician, had assembled his acolytes in a room that none of them had ever visited in the underbelly of the castle. It was cold, dark, and very wet. Brön could distinctly hear the rustling of rodents in their immediate vicinity. He shuddered at the thought.

Niels extended a hand to him and reached for the leather water bag that Brön had used to carry the Witches' blood from Norway.

"This is the blood of Witches," he said raising the bag for all to see. Most of the physicians gasped and recoiled.

"We are tasked with studying it and reporting our findings to the King," he stated.

"For what purpose?"

"It is assumed that the hags made a pact with the devil, and so their children were spared. But the King believes, as do I, that these women are cursed at birth and so are all in their bloodline. So, by studying it, if we can find something in their blood that is different from our blood, then all Witches can be hunted down and eliminated."

The men nodded, understanding. One of the men spoke the thought that many of them hadn't dared. "Niels, why could you not discuss this in the surgery?" he asked.

"This matter must be handled with the utmost secrecy. No one outside this room, other than the King, of course, is to know about our experiments or their outcomes," Niels warned.

The acolytes nodded gravely.

"In fact, you must swear it here and now. Should you break your vow, the King will have your families slaughtered."

In quick succession, the six physicians were sworn to secrecy. Niels poured samples of blood into corked glass vials and passed them around.

"Take pains to hide your experiments and your findings. We shall meet here every week until we have conclusive evidence for the King," said Niels before dismissing them.

Brön pocketed a vial, bowed to Niels, and left the chamber. This was an interesting turn of events. If he could be the one to cure the world from the plague of Witches, the King would reward him handsomely.

CHAPTER

ONE

TOM, Zaina, and Arturo debated Tom's suggestion that they needed to get help. After Mandy had been kidnapped and taken to what was presumably The Master's lair, the trio had followed her trail, intent on rescuing her as soon as possible.

As it was, the small castle was under heavy guard. It was also surrounded by a ten-foot stone wall and wards preventing anyone who might chance a climb, or a hover, as Arturo had attempted, from getting in.

They had located Mandy using Tom's Traveling Door. Even if there hadn't been wards, they wouldn't have been able to open a Door to Mandy's exact location. Travelers could not open Doors into private homes or crowded public places like museums or outdoor events.

"When you say, 'get help,' do you mean from the teachers or some of our other friends?" asked Zaina. Despite being outwardly brusque with Mandy, and everyone really, she couldn't hide the fact that she had a soft spot for the weak and the oppressed.

Tom shrugged.

"I mean... the teachers at Harding are pretty chill, and they probably have more experience than the students. Honestly, I trust *you* guys," referring to his new Harding friends, "but I'm not sure about the rest. This is my fight, and I can't ask anyone to risk their lives in good conscience," he replied.

"You didn't ask for our help," replied Zaina.

"Exactly! I couldn't stop you from coming, and I sure can't make you do anything you don't want to do. But there's no way the three of us can go in there and get Mandy without running into an army of Warlocks. We can't do it alone."

"Tom's right. You and I are the strongest, most powerful students at Harding. We need help from people who know what they're up against and how to deal with it. Besides, the whole faculty will be up in arms by now. They must already be planning a rescue. One of the students was taken from the school grounds; I'd be surprised if they haven't already contacted Mandy's parents as well as the CEMB," said Arturo.

"They don't know Mandy's been abducted. All they know is that *four* students disappeared into a sinkhole. When Benny left, Mandy, Tom, and I were in the hole. When they don't find any of us in there, all hell will break loose," said Zaina.

"Crap. You're right. What if they call my mom? I don't think she can take another traumatic event. We have to go back. Now! Let's go!" said Tom, pulling out his Key.

"Fine," conceded Zaina, turning to look at the castle. She looked worried but also pissed off. "Let's go before they send a search party, and we lose the element of surprise."

Tom opened a Door and they stepped out in front of the main school entrance. They'd been gone for no more than twenty minutes, but already the school was buzzing with chatter about the sinkhole. They were getting looks as they walked down the hall to the Head-mistress's office.

They found Benny standing just outside the door, his ear pressed against it.

"What's going on?" asked Zaina.

Benny's face lit up when he saw them. He immediately moved toward Tom and gave him a big hug. "I'm so happy to see you! We thought you'd been kidnapped!" he said moving to Zaina. The look she gave him kept him from embracing her, and he patted her awkwardly on the shoulder. Arturo put out a fist and Benny gave it a bump. "Where's Mandy?"

Arturo ignored the question and asked one of his own. "They think we've been kidnapped?" he repeated.

"Um, yeah. Sorry. After I saw you, I got Miss Clementine. She and a few teachers came to investigate since the wards should have kept anyone with evil intentions out. When we got to the hole and they saw the tunnel, they understood how the perimeter had been breached. The wards only protect us above ground. Anyway, when we couldn't locate any of you, teachers spread out over the grounds and inside the school to ensure that there weren't any other tunnels leading into the school. They didn't find any other tunnels, but as you were still missing, they've been arguing about what to do ever since..."

"Gotcha," replied Zaina. "Sorry for bailing Benny, but we didn't want to lose Mandy's trail."

"What do you mean by 'Mandy's trail'? Where is she? Was she hurt? Is she at the infirmary?" asked Benny, eyes wild, searching the halls for their missing friend.

"We think The Master took her. We know where she is, but we're going to need help getting her out of there," replied Tom. "Come on, Benny you can hear about it when the teachers do," he said, as Tom and his friends hurried to Miss Clementine's office.

Tom knocked on the door. The voices immediately grew quiet, and Lady Mathilda opened the door.

She put a hand to her heart and exhaled in relief. "Thank heavens you're safe," she said upon seeing them. "Come in, come in," she ushered them in, resting a hand on each of their heads as they passed through. "Where's Mandy?"

She escorted them inside Miss Clementine's office. Tom had only been there twice before. Once when he'd registered with his mum and another time when he'd shared memories with Miss Clementine, Professor Montague, and Professor Bellamy. It was much larger than the other offices Tom had been to at Harding Academy.

Miss Clementine's work desk was set in an alcove at the far-right corner of the room. During the day, the floor-to-ceiling windows provided ample natural lighting from the southeastern exposure. Tonight, there was only a sliver of moonlight.

The Headmistress was seated with some teachers in her large sitting room at the front of her office. This was where she held informal meetings with staff, parents, and students. She said it made people more comfortable than facing her at her desk. It was indeed a cozy setup.

At present, Professors Hilltop, Bellamy, and Montague were in attendance and they looked anything but comfortable.

She rose when Tom and his friends entered. When Tom was about to explain, she held out her hand, "This will be faster, I believe." Tom placed his hand in the tiny Witch's palm and closed his eyes. He focused on the evening's events.

Miss Clementine released his hand and, before Tom had opened his eyes, she had moved on to Zaina, then Arturo.

"Have a seat, won't you?" she said gesturing behind her as she called Lady Mathilda. The High Elf rose and came to clasp hands with the Headmistress. Likely, the High Elf had read their minds as she placed a hand on their heads when they first came in. Tom wondered if she'd gotten anything out of him since he hadn't purposely given her access.

Lady Mathilda and Miss Clementine stood together and nodded, unclasping their hands. Tom knew that Lady Mathilda would share the information she had gathered with Headmaster Lianon and any other relevant High Elf such as those who sat on the CEMB.

Miss Clementine invited all in attendance to join hands and asked Professor Bellamy to show them the highlights. High Elves could also share their knowledge with others through touch. If the group held hands, everyone would get the information. However, it worked best with simple facts. For this, having Professor Bellamy take them through the events would help them re-enact and observe them in greater detail.

The memories started them off in the field. Everyone saw the fire circle drop six feet below ground. Then, the service station where they saw Mandy driving off. Finally, they were transported in their mind's eye to the castle. The scene kept shifting between Tom's point of view, Zaina's, and Arturo's bird's eye view.

Zaina shot Tom a look that captured exactly how Tom felt; it was super creepy to look through each other's eyes. However, it gave everyone an excellent overview of the location.

"Does anyone know where this is?" inquired Miss Clementine.

No one had seen the castle before. "Mathilda, can you ask the High Elves about the location?" Miss Clementine asked. Lady Mathilda nodded and closed her eyes for a moment and came back, shaking her head no. It was fascinating to see that High Elves could communicate through telepathy so quickly, and across worlds. Though the CEMB was based in London, The Academy, and The Summer Iles, the High Elves' homeland, were on different worlds entirely.

"Have you called our parents?" asked Tom with a gulp.

Miss Clementine and Lady Mathilda exchanged a look. The teachers shifted in their seats, cleared their throats, and avoided eye contact.

"Not yet dear. As it's been less than an hour, we thought it best to ensure you were actually missing before we made any hasty phone calls."

"Right, but now that you know Mandy's been abducted, surely you'll call her parents to let them know."

"As Mandy is of age, we are not required to inform her parents if she misses curfew," replied Miss Clementine, giving Lady Mathilda a sidelong glance.

Zaina looked at Tom, Arturo, and then at Miss Clementine. "She's not out at the village pub!" retorted Zaina, getting up from her seat. "She's been taken by an evil Sorcerer!"

Lady Mathilda came to Zaina's side and rested a hand on the girl's shoulder. Her calm and patient reply would have mollified most students. But not Zaina. She stared up at the beautiful High Elf with her jaw set and her arms crossed.

"We searched the school and the grounds as soon as Benny came to tell us. We also sent faculty members to the village and the area surrounding the school. As Miss Clementine said, she's been gone less than an hour. We can't call the authorities until she's been missing for forty-eight hours."

At this point, Professor Hilltop stood up. "The tunnel was collapsed. We pushed through the debris to make sure you weren't stuck on the other side. There was no sign of struggle. When we couldn't locate any of you, we assumed you'd used Tom's Door."

"You didn't actually see her being taken by The Master, did you?" asked Professor Montague, who had remained quiet until now.

"Well, no," replied Zaina, her bravado slipping a little.

"While I agree The Master has to be involved, the only thing you saw was a man that looked like a mole dig a tunnel across the field and come out of the earth at the other end. And both he and Mandy got into a black automobile. Correct?" asked Professor Hilltop.

Tom and Zaina looked at Arturo who only shrugged. He'd never mentioned that Mandy's abductor had looked like a mole, but Tom guessed it made sense if he was able to dig a tunnel that fast under a five-hundred-foot field.

"That's correct," replied Arturo when no one else spoke up.

"I suggest we get cracking on a locator spell while we wait for news from the CEMB," said Professor Montague heading for the table they had used when Tom had been there last.

She checked her antique watch and said, "Zaina, would you go to Mandy's room and tell her roommate that she's unwell and staying in the infirmary tonight and that you are collecting a few things for her? That should kill two birds with one stone."

Zaina looked reluctant to leave. But she did as her teacher had asked.

"Benny, dear, would you go to my classroom and fetch the box that's in the bottom right-hand drawer?" she said next.

"Yes, Professor," replied Benny and left the room at a run.

While Professor Montague was setting up, Miss Clementine asked Tom and Arturo to accompany Professor Hilltop to the sinkhole so that it may be put to rights. Now that everyone was accounted for, they didn't want any more students to fall in and injure themselves.

"But why do we need to go with Professor Hilltop?" asked Tom.

"So you can learn the spell of course," she replied with a smile.

Tom looked to Arturo. "Do you know the spell to *un*sink a hole?"

"I believe I do," he replied smugly.

"Then you know it's best performed by two or more Warlocks," said Professor Hilltop, holding the door open and nodding for them to follow him out.

CHAPTER
TWO

TOM FOLLOWED Professor Hilltop and Arturo out the main entrance and back to the scene of the crime. He couldn't shake the feeling that Professor Montague wanted to get rid of them and wished he could be a fly on the wall to hear the conversation after they'd left the room.

Professor Hilltop had them space out around the hole and extend their arms. He'd written the spell on a piece of paper for Tom to memorize. It wasn't difficult and focusing on the spell took his mind off his other worries.

"First, gather your energy in your belly. Then, send it out through your hands, as though reaching for mine and Arturo's. This will create a circle of power we can leverage to raise the fallen plot of land back into position."

Tom followed the directions but was disappointed when he couldn't feel the rush of energy he expected. Nonetheless, the fire pit rose slowly as the ground he stood on shook until it was level with the rest of the grass. Then, it settled. When Tom looked down, he could no longer see the line where the section had torn off. It was like it had never happened. Gingerly, he placed a foot on it and pressed down. It held.

"You can put your arms down, Tom. We're done," said Arturo. He was smiling at Tom, amused to see him walking, then jumping around on the grass.

"I don't think I was any help," he said to Professor Hilltop. "I didn't feel any energy coming out of me."

"Likely, your main gift is your Blood Magick. But everyone can send energy and hold an intention. Even if they don't have magic," replied the Professor.

Tom nodded, it made sense. He'd been able to use spells in class and he hadn't felt any strange sensations, not like when he drew on his Blood Magick. He continued to mull things over in his mind as they walked back to the Headmistress' office.

"Arturo?" asked Tom, as a thought occurred to him.

Arturo had been chatting with Professor Hilltop and turned back, stopping when he saw Tom pause. "Yeah?"

"Did you read the books about Blood Magick?"

"I looked through them," he replied, motioning for Tom to walk with him.

"Did any of them say where it came from?" asked Tom.

At this, Professor Hilltop slowed his pace and fell into step with the boys.

"I believe I can answer that question," he said. "After you were incapacitated by the charmed bracelet, I did a bit of research myself. In fact, I asked Arturo to go over some of the books with you, since I'd seen you two together."

"I want to be Professor Hilltop's teaching assistant next year," replied Arturo with a shrug.

"It seems you never got a chance to look at them," replied the teacher.

"No, Sir. I was planning on meeting Arturo at the library, but I was detained," Tom admitted.

"Yes, of course. Well, from what I gathered, the earliest reference to Blood Magick was found in 1670, when King Frederick died. When King Christian was crowned, they found secret correspondence between King Frederick and his head physician. The physician had found conclusive evidence that Witches were born with magic and could pass it on to their offspring. He created a secret task force of special Witch Hunters trained to identify a Witch by the taste of their blood. They found ledgers filled with the names of Witches that had been executed quietly on the King's orders."

"That's terrible!" exclaimed Tom, feeling sick to his stomach. He knew about the Witch trials, everybody did. But this was a level he'd not been aware of. "I'm sorry, Sir, I can't recall a King Frederick…"

"He was the King of Denmark and Norway. The Vardo Witch Trials were some of the most gruesome in Europe. The fact that King Frederick assembled a clandestine team to pursue Witches after the trials had concluded is one of the greatest horrors I've ever read about."

Arturo and Tom nodded. "What happened then?" asked Tom

"King Christian called the Witch Hunters back to the castle since they had spread out across the land, some taking their quest into Sweden and Finland. Those who came back were executed for vigilante justice. Though their actions were secretly sanctioned by the King, the accused, whether they were Witches, thieves, or murderers, were entitled to a trial before their peers."

"How many returned?" asked Tom.

"Only one did not return. And he was never found. For ten years, the King searched for the missing Witch Hunter. He was presumed dead, and the matter closed."

"But he wasn't dead!" jumped in Arturo.

"What happened to him?" prodded Tom.

"The Witch Hunter's fate is more lore than fact," hedged Professor Hilltop.

"Tell me!" said Tom, a little too loudly.

"They say that instead of killing the Witches after he tested their blood, he would drink their blood to absorb their power," replied Arturo.

Tom tripped and made a grab for Arturo's robe to steady himself.

"You mean, like a vampire?" he barely managed to reply.

"No. He would bleed them to death, collect a bit of their blood, and drink it."

Tom put a hand over his mouth. He was going to be sick.

Am I that man's descendant?

Oblivious to Tom's discomfort, Arturo continued.

"Legend has it that a Witch managed to curse him before she died."

"What did she curse him with?" Tom asked warily.

"Until he got a Witch to fall in love with him, and he loved her in return, he would never again enjoy human pleasures," replied Professor Hilltop.

"You mean..." said Tom, pumping his eyebrows.

"Get your mind out of the gutter! He meant food, drink, sleep, you name it," replied Arturo.

"So, she basically turned him into a vampire!" Tom replied, confused.

"No! He could still do all that, but he couldn't enjoy it and he was never satisfied. For example, food would have been tasteless, and he'd leave the table still hungry even after eating a huge meal."

"Huh," replied Tom. That still sounded like a vampire to Tom. They were never satisfied until they drank blood; if they even existed, that is.

When they reached Miss Clementine's door, Tom asked, "Did he ever break the curse?"

"No one knows for sure," replied Professor Hilltop, "but he must have because the last known Blood Mage, before you that is, was never described as being anything but a powerful Sorcerer. Feared, yes. But evil? No."

CHAPTER
THREE

BACK INSIDE, Professor Montague and Zaina were casting a locator spell over a huge map of the UK. Benny stood by a stack of books with alternate maps. They'd apparently started with a map of the world, then Europe. Narrowing the search further, another map put Mandy in Scotland, a mere thirty minutes away by car, though no roads seemed to lead into the dense forest.

"That's a relief," said Miss Clementine. "At least she's nearby."

Seeing that the boys had returned, she told them to have a seat. They were waiting on Lady Mathilda who had gone to the CEMB headquarters to ask for their input. Professor Bellamy rang for a late tea, and everyone took turns saying how they thought they should proceed.

"I say we send Tom to their front door. The minions won't harm him; they'll take him straight to The Master," suggested Zaina.

"You mean like bait?" asked Tom.

"No, like a distraction," said Arturo, catching on.

"But what about the wards?" asked Benny.

"We can handle the wards," replied Professor Hilltop. "And most of the outside guards."

"How are you going to fight all the guards? They're posted at every door," said Tom.

Professor Montague shook her head in dismay. "We may be old, but we're not ineffectual. We don't need to fight them, only incapacitate them long enough to retrieve the girl."

"Professor Montague is right. Leave the outer guards to us. We have more than a spell or two up our sleeves," said Professor Hilltop with a wink.

There was a knock at the door and Professor Bellamy rose to answer it. It was Holly, the kitchen girl who Tom had accidentally healed when they were testing his powers. When she saw Tom, she paused, momentarily stunned. Tom gave her an awkward wave, she smiled briefly and turned back to the task at hand.

She rolled the tea trolley to the seating area and placed the tray on the table, then arranged some plates with an assortment of finger foods and treats. Once she'd unloaded the trolley, she gave a half-curtsy to no one in particular and left the room.

"A friend of yours?" asked Zaina.

"It's a long story," replied Tom.

As everyone was digging into the impromptu snack, Professor Bellamy spoke up.

"You said you kept returning to the same spot with your Door. That likely means Mandy is being held on that side of the castle. Once the wards are down, I could create an illusion to keep the guards busy while you hover and look through the windows. Once you've spotted her, it should be simple enough to get in through the window."

"But won't she be under guard?" asked Benny.

"That's where you come in. While the guards are busy and away from their posts, you'll enter and make your way to the room where they're holding Mandy. On your way, you'll immobilize anyone you come into contact with," explained Professor Bellamy.

"But it doesn't usually last very long," replied Benny.

"You only need to freeze them long enough to pass by. One of us will follow you in and take care of the ruffians," answered Professor Montague.

"I'll wait with Mandy until you come and get us," said Arturo. "If there's someone in there with her, I think I can take care of them."

"What about me?" asked Tom.

"You'll be stalling The Master. Make him believe you've come to join ranks with him if he releases Mandy unharmed."

"I'd feel better if we knew more about the place. In all the spy movies, they have blueprints and know where all the airshafts are," said Benny.

Tom laughed, more out of nervousness than humor. Benny was right. They were going in blind.

"I'll do you one better, young Benny. I'll astral project there like I did when Tabitha was kidnapped. When I come back, I can share what I've seen with Professor Bellamy and she'll show everyone," offered Professor Montague.

"In that case, why can't Lady Mathilda Portal in, grab Mandy, and get out?" asked Tom.

"One, she's not back yet. Two, I'm not sure she can get through the wards. Three, she needs to be on standby to get you out if things go south," said Zaina.

"Zaina is correct. She is also the only one who can quickly call for help through telepathy, should we become woefully outnumbered," added Professor Hilltop.

"But if it's so dangerous, why don't we let the CEMB go in and get her," said Benny.

"It's not their responsibility. They're tasked with ensuring magical humans don't misuse magic or expose us to non-magical humans. Theirs is more of an investigative role," replied Miss Clementine.

"Student safety is the school's responsibility unless it's a non-magical issue. Then, we would call the authorities. But as previously mentioned, Mandy hasn't been missing for forty-eight hours."

"Right then. It's time for a little recognizance," said Professor Montague as she headed for what had to be Miss Clementine's ritual space. As far as Tom could tell, it looked a lot like a meditation corner. The area was separated from the rest of the room with a bead curtain. Behind it, Tom saw a small wooden altar, bare at the moment, and a large circular cushion on the ground. To the right was a low bookcase filled with assorted candles, stones, mirrors, tied herbs, and other small objects Tom couldn't identify from where he stood.

Professor Montague went through the beads, turned her back to them, sent her robes flying out behind her, and sank gracefully onto the cushion. She did not rearrange herself or shift for comfort. She was immediately still.

All the others could do was wait. Arturo's foot was tapping the floor and Zaina was picking unconsciously at her cuticles. Benny was eating while both Professor Hilltop and Professor Bellamy seemed to be napping, likely projecting. Miss Clementine had moved to her office to make a phone call.

Tom was thinking back to Arturo's tale about the last Witch Hunter. Had he broken the curse? How and when had he done it? His father's journal had labeled Blood Magick as dangerous, but not evil, and advised the reader to seek out Petunia Eva.

When Tom had visited Petunia and her twin sister in the past, he and his friends had found no answers there. Perhaps they'd gone too far back. They'd gone in 1667 when the twins were younger, unmarried.

"Arturo, do you know what year King Frederick died? How long after the Witch trials?" asked Tom.

Arturo puffed out a breath and squinted, trying to recall the information. "I believe the Vardo Witch Trials ended in 1663 and King Frederick died in 1670."

"Thanks," said Tom absently. Petunia had met and married Sir Anthony Callahan while he was in Virginia. Tom couldn't' recall the date of their marriage. They moved to Ireland and had three sons. Conor, Tom's ancestor, was born in 1685. He inherited the lands and title after his brother died of influenza.

When the Portal opened, everyone but Professor Montague jumped. Lady Mathilda came through, but she wasn't alone.

"You!" shouted Tom. "What are you doing here? *Alistair*, is it? Or do you prefer *Emmett*?" snorted Tom.

"Tom, I can explain," Alistair said, holding his hands up like Tom was waving a gun at him.

The Portal closed and everyone sat to hear what Alistair had to say. Before he began, Lady Mathilda introduced him.

"For those who don't know him, this is Alistair Callahan. He is a former student of Harding Academy, currently working for the MFO. He also happens to be Tom's second cousin; their grandfathers were twin brothers. Brian, Alistair's grandfather, attended school here, but Brandon did not. He chose to attend The Academy, where Tom went to school before joining us here. Are we all caught up?"

Zaina, Benny, and Arturo were casting wild glances at Tom who could merely shrug and nod.

"Thank you, Lady Mathilda," Alistair said and bowed.

"That is correct," he continued. "Last Saturday, I came to Harding to see Tom. I'm afraid I had to use subterfuge to attain my goal: retrieve the Callahan ring. I'm sorry for it, Tom. Truly, I am. I would have hoped to meet you under different circumstances."

Alistair gave Tom an earnest look, but Tom was reserving judgment until he heard the whole story. He nodded for Alistair to continue.

"A few weeks ago, the CEMB approached me with an unusual request. In my work at the Magical Foreign Office, I am often required to assume a different identity so we can apprehend the culprits we are investigating."

"You're very skilled," said Tom dryly. Alistair gave him a pained smile and resumed his tale. "The CEMB wanted me to infiltrate The Master's operation, not under an alias, but as myself."

"Why?" asked Zaina.

"Because I'm a Callahan and I might be useful in luring Tom to the dark side, so to speak," he replied.

"But that makes no sense! I didn't know you even existed until two days ago. Why would that make any difference to The Master?" asked Tom, utterly confused.

"The story I was going to use to get in was that my father was dying, and I heard The Master could cure him and I was ready to do anything. That would get me in the door. The CEMB thought that once

The Master knew there was a connection between Tom and me, he would want to exploit it. And that's exactly what happened."

"Wait, so you're saying The Master told you to come to school, pretend to be Emmett, and steal my ring?" asked Tom.

"No. He assigned me other tasks. But I heard him talking to one of his minions about the ring and how it was making you angry and paranoid. The Master was sure you'd be easier to sway if you'd lost confidence in yourself and those around you," Alistair explained.

"It was working," said Tom, scratching the back of his head. He was still embarrassed at the stupid things he'd said and done while under the influence of the ring. "What did you do with the ring?"

"It's still here at Harding. I tied it to one of the cat's collars in the cellar," he replied, smiling at his own ingenuity.

"That's a terrible thing to do to a poor defenseless animal!" cried Benny.

"Don't worry, it can't harm a cat, only a Witch or Warlock. Besides, I had to put it somewhere that would give the illusion that Tom was still wearing it at Harding, in case The Master could track it somehow."

"That was clever of you," said Miss Clementine, beaming at her former pupil.

"Thanks," said Alistair, beaming back at her.

At that moment, Professor Montague rose from the cushion and joined them.

"Alistair! How lovely to see you again," she exclaimed upon seeing the young man.

"It's a pleasure to be here, Professor Montague."

"Right, then. Mathilda, I'm glad you're back. I've just come back from The Master's lair and I'm ready to share what I've seen. You'll all be happy to know that Mandy is safe and unharmed. You'll see for yourself in a moment."

They all joined hands again. As Professor Montague took them around the castle, up the stairs, and to the room where they were holding Mandy, Alistair provided extra details that would be useful when they stormed the castle.

Mandy was in a small bedroom, tied to a chair with her hands behind her back with a gag in her mouth. Her eyes were closed, giving the illusion that she was sleeping, but her head wasn't lolling or hanging in slumber.

"That poor girl," whimpered Professor Bellamy.

"They hadn't tied or gagged her at first, but she kept trying to freeze everyone and cast spells," explained Alistair.

"She looks like she's hatching a plan," said Zaina, rubbing her hands together in anticipation.

"Can Mandy astral project? Could she be here, now?" asked Tom, looking around the room and waving, just in case. Benny burst out laughing and Zaina just shook her head in disbelief.

"I don't know how much practice she's had, but all students learn how to do it," replied Professor Montague.

"Even if she's here, or has been here, there's not much we can do about it since her body is trapped at the castle. At least she'll know we've located her and are preparing an extraction," said Arturo.

If Tom didn't know better, he'd think Arturo was enjoying himself. Of course, he wasn't happy that Mandy was kidnapped, or that a raving lunatic had her. But Tom could see that planning and implementation is where Arturo truly shined. He'd make a great team leader.

It occurred to Tom that everyone in the room knew who they were. His friends and teachers all seemed to know their own strengths and weaknesses. It was time for Tom to get a clue. As the others were running through the amended plan to include the intel Alistair had provided, Tom kept thinking about the last Witch Hunter. The more he thought about it, the more he felt like some more Time Walking was in order. He should go back to see Petunia, only later. After she'd already married and had children.

If he had more time, he would go home to his father's study and read all his journals. Surely, he'd written more about Petunia some-where. When Time Walking, Travelers came back at the exact moment they left. If Lola were willing, they could go back in time, say before his birthday party last August. They could spend the day looking for more information about Petunia. Then again, if they did that, how would that change the trip they'd taken with Professor Ballantyne earlier this year? Tom shook his head, it was too confusing to think about. And besides, Lola wouldn't agree.

Professor Ballantyne, however, might agree to take Tom to see Petunia again. If Lady Mathilda communicated telepathically with Headmaster Lianon, it could be arranged in less than 10 minutes. Tom would take a Door to The Academy where Professor Ballantyne would be waiting. They'd go, find their answers and no time would have elapsed, save the time it took to get to and from The Academy. Twenty minutes tops.

"I have an idea," exclaimed Tom, getting up from the sofa.

CHAPTER
FOUR

THERE WAS some debate over Tom's plan. In the end, the teachers agreed since it wouldn't take too long, and it could provide helpful information.

Professor Hilltop was selected to accompany Tom as the Offensive Magic teacher, even though Professor Ballantyne could likely keep Tom safe.

Tom was pretty sure that the teacher was more intent on taking a trip to the past than on offering his protection. Tom couldn't blame him. It was a really cool thing to do.

When they got to Professor Ballantyne's classroom, she was ready for them. She thrust some appropriate clothes at them, introduced herself briskly to the other teacher, and flipped open the Time Watch as she took out her Key. She was already dressed in mid-seventeenth-century attire.

"We'll be arriving a few weeks after Conor's birth. That should place Petunia at home with the baby. She may recognize us from our previous trip; that would be helpful. Remember, we don't need to rush once we're there, as we'll be back here at the same time we left," she explained. "Ready?"

Tom and Professor Hilltop nodded. Professor Ballantyne had a look through the window; the coast was clear, and they stepped into 1685 Ireland.

"WE'LL BE a married couple traveling with our son if anybody asks," whispered Professor Ballantyne.

"In that case, I think it's fitting that you call me Alfred," replied Professor Hilltop in hushed tones. They had arrived just outside the gates to the Estate. Since they had neither horse nor carriage, they entered through the side door and headed toward the main entrance.

"You can call me Chaundra."

"Mother Chaundra, how do we get past the servants?" asked Tom sweetly. Petunia had married very well indeed. The Callahan Estate, in the Wicklow Mountains, was impressive and the house was large enough to require a full staff.

"I'll tell the butler that we are friends from the Colonies come for a visit," suggested Professor Ballantyne. They were almost at the front steps. "Don't worry, I'm great at improv."

They went up and pulled the bell. Many minutes later, the door was opened not by a well-dressed butler, but by a red-faced housekeeper.

"Cad atá uait?" she said, wiping her hands on her dirty apron.

Professors Ballantyne and Hilltop looked at one another, then back at the lady.

Tom chuckled.

"Táimid anseo chun mo Aintín Petunia a fheiceáil. Táimid ar cuairt ó na coilíneachtaí," Tom said to the housekeeper in his rudimentary Irish. She grunted and stepped aside, closing the heavy door behind them.

She led them to a parlor and bade them sit by the fire. It was a bit late to be receiving visitors, but as Tom had told her they were visiting their aunt from the Colonies, a late arrival might not be too suspicious.

All three of them sat on the settee, hands folded neatly on their laps. Tom looked at the furnishings in the room. They looked expensive and he wondered if anything from here had been passed down to his family. Tom's family certainly hadn't inherited the Estate.

They heard someone coming and rose in unison when a lady entered the room. Tom recognized her at once. While not a handsome woman, Petunia had aged well. She looked happy and healthy.

She took in the strangers one by one, starting with Professor Hilltop. She smiled pleasantly and moved to Professor Ballantyne. Her smile wavered as their eyes met. Petunia squinted, trying to place the woman in her parlor. Next, she looked at Tom.

The smile returned and she rushed toward him. "Tom! You've come back!"

"Yes Miss Harding, I mean Mrs. O'Callahan," Tom said. He wondered if she should be addressed as My Lady or some such since she'd married Sir Anthony.

"And you!" she said looking at Professor Ballantyne, relaxing now that she had identified her.

"We apologize for the subterfuge, but we wanted to be sure you'd see us at such a late hour," replied Tom's teacher. "This is Alfred, another of Tom's professors."

Professor Hilltop bowed. "It's a pleasure to meet you, Lady O' Callahan."

She smiled and invited them to sit down.

"I would have been pleased to see any of my sister's children, but I doubt they'll ever make the journey to the mainland," she said as she asked if they wanted tea.

Professor Ballantyne declined and got to the point.

"Tom has some questions. He may divulge aspects of the future when asking them. Are you comfortable with that?"

"I... yes, of course. I wouldn't believe he'd come all this way if it wasn't important," she replied.

"Quite so," said Professor Hilltop.

Tom cleared his throat and tried to word his question in his mind. Should he preface it with the current situation? Should he tell her about Blood Magick?

"Lady O'Callahan, on our last visit, we asked about your magical abilities. Both you and your sister have abilities much like Lola and Devlin, the friends that accompanied us on our last visit. However, I have manifested entirely different abilities. They call it Blood Magick in our time," he said and paused to let her respond.

A hand flew to her mouth, and she gasped. "In this time, they call it Satan-worshiping!" she exclaimed.

Tom looked at his teachers for guidance. Professor Hilltop nodded for him to continue.

"It is safe to assume I inherited the abilities from one of your descendants. As I clearly did not get them from you," Tom suggested.

Petunia crossed herself, fished out a rosary from her pocket, and fingered the beads.

Placing a hand on Tom's shoulder, Professor Hilltop spoke next.

"Have you ever heard about a cursed Witch Hunter? Legend has it, he was cursed to live a half-life until he could fall in love with a Witch and gain her love in return. Only then would the curse be lifted."

Petunia dropped the rosary to the ground as she shot up out of the armchair. She was wringing her hands, tears welling up in her eyes. She walked to the parlor door, checked the hall, and closed it. There was a distinct click as she turned the key in the lock before returning to sit.

She placed her face in her hands and wept. Tom and his teachers were at a loss. What did it mean? At the very least, she knew about the Witch Hunter. Professor Ballantyne rose to hand her a handkerchief, placing a comforting hand on Petunia's shoulder.

Petunia thanked her and dabbed at her eyes and nose. She took a few steadying breaths before she could speak.

"I am the Witch who broke the curse."

CHAPTER
FIVE

PETUNIA PLAYED with the handkerchief for a moment, lost in thought. Finally, she looked up and began her tale.

"The voyage from the Colonies was long and challenging. It was a cargo ship returning to Ireland after delivering its shipment of enslaved Irish people, pardoned prisoners who would be sold as indentured servants to wealthy settlers.

I was a naive girl, knowing nothing of how the world worked. Papa had encouraged the match to the prosperous Sir Anthony. Rose had just wed Lord Evers, and she was so pleased, that I assumed I would enjoy the same marital bliss as she.

The journey was made uncomfortable by the rigors of the sea, dismal accommodations, and inadequate sustenance. It was made unbearable by the discoveries I made about my new husband.

Though wealthy and titled, with impeccable manners and a handsome face, the man I married was anything but genteel. Perhaps he was like every other wealthy landowner. My papa was a kind and patient man who treated everyone with respect. I assumed, wrongly, that all men were like him.

I will not bore you with the tale of my marital woes. Suffice it to say, that once he had dispatched his martial duty and established me as the Lady of the house, Sir Anthony departed on another journey, only to return months later.

I spoke Norwegian and English, but not Irish. Communicating with the staff was laborious, and there were no close neighbors. It was very isolating. I hoped Sir Anthony had left me with child, but when my courses came, melancholy slowly set in.

One day, a man came to the house seeking shelter. He spoke English with an accent I immediately recognized. He was Norwegian!

Curious, I came out of the parlor to hear Mabel telling him to go around back to the kitchen, and she'd find a bed for him in the stables. It was plain that he had been living rough for some time from his attire. He was dirty and unshaven.

However, he did not speak like a vagrant. He sounded like a learned man. I immediately told Mabel to let my kinsman inside.

In English, I introduced myself as Lady O'Callahan and welcomed him to Sir Anthony's home. I apologized that my husband was away but told him he could rest here for a few days before resuming his journey.

I asked Mabel to prepare a room, a bath, and some food for the man called Brön.

I did not see him again that day, but I chanced upon him at the stables the next morning, saddling his horse. I was heading out for my morning ride and asked if he wished to accompany me. At first, he refused, saying he didn't wasn't to intrude on my solitude. That made me laugh."

"Truth be told, my Lady, I had planned on resuming my journey. I thank you for your hospitality, but I think it best if I were on my way," he had said.

He was clean and shaven, and I could see he had laundered his clothes though they hadn't yet dried fully. He looked more than presentable, though he still seemed pale and haggard.

"I assure you I've had more than enough of my solitude, Sir. It would be a refreshing change to converse with someone from my homeland," I entreated.

He considered my request for a moment and replied, "Very well. It would not be very gentlemanly to let a Lady ride alone over these savage fields."

"I usually take a groom with me, but I appreciate the sentiment," I said as my horse was brought out and I mounted. "Shall we?"

I took him around the Estate, pointing out different pleasant features. We paused by the lake to rest our mounts.

"How odd for you to have traveled from Norway to the Colonies, only to return married to an Irishman," he said.

"Indeed! Have been away from home for long? What news have you to share?"

He explained that he'd been the King's head physician, sent on a mission when the King died. Suddenly without a purpose, he'd ventured out into the world, tending wounds and helping the sick, as he went from village to village.

I was immediately wary when he said he'd been King Frederick's physician. The Witch hunts were the reason we fled Norway in the first place. However, as he spoke of the people he had attended in his travels, and the other healers he had met, I decided he wasn't a threat.

We resumed our ride and I opened up to him about my own healing abilities. The only people I cared for at the time were the household staff. As there were so many of them, it kept me busy enough.

"The Irish are a superstitious lot. I didn't dare suggest anything other than teas and salves at first, for fear they'd label me a Witch!" I had confided in him.

"Yes, people are rather ignorant. It takes a keen eye to recognize a true Witch," he replied rather cryptically, and I immediately regretted speaking up.

As we rode back to the stables, I steered our conversation to safer topics by asking where he'd been on his travels. When we returned to the stables, I reiterated my offer to have him spend a few more days. It was more out of politeness, though I admit to enjoying the company, even if he unsettled me. There was something so engaging about him.

He surprised me by suggesting that he would attend to the staff while he was here.

"I don't doubt your skill, but I'm sure your servants would prefer being tended by a true physician than by their employer," he said.

I should have been insulted, but I knew he meant well. While I was a skilled healer, I was also their mistress, and it wasn't befitting my station.

For the next few days, he met with each household staff member. He'd set up his clinic in one of the rooms near the kitchen we used for storing food after the harvest. As it was May, it was almost empty.

We rode together in the morning and dined together at night. We had so much to talk about on the topic of healing, books, and Norway. I began to dread the day he would leave, and I would once again be starved for attention and conversation.

On the fourth morning, I expected him to say he was leaving. He'd packed his belongings and we left for our morning ride as usual. As we rode, I realized I had grown to care for him in a way that was less than was proper. When we stopped to rest the horses by the lake, he picked a rose and gave me the flower. I was charmed beyond belief and started to think he cared for me too.

I pricked my finger on a thorn and he was by my side in an instant. What he did next can hardly be repeated in good company, but as it has bearing on the tale, I'll have to divulge it.

He placed my bleeding finger in his mouth. Though I was both horrified at his familiarity, I was unable to pull my finger from his grasp. Though we'd shared many personal remarks in our discussions, we had always remained at a respectable distance. The intimacy of this act felt far more profound than sharing the marital bed with my husband. I was appalled, yet thrilled, at the thought.

The moment was fleeting, for his eyes grew wide and he dropped my hand like I was Satan himself.

"You're a Witch!" he accused, stepping back from me. His expression was hard to decipher. He should have been frightened, or angry in his accusation. But his face held pain, confusion, and anguish.

Before I knew what was happening, he grabbed my arm, swung me around, and held a knife to my throat.

"The King doesn't suffer Witches and neither do I," he hissed.

I was stunned into silence, unable to find words to defend myself, let alone plead for my life. Truth be told, he could take it. I had been unhappy for too long and had clearly misjudged the one man I thought was my salvation.

I closed my eyes and accepted my fate. They say you can't outrun your destiny and mine had been sealed on the shores of Finnmark when I was born a Witch.

I waited for death, but it didn't come. Brön wasn't slicing my throat, he was kissing it. We...consummated our affection."

Petunia rose and went to stand in front of the fireplace. Tom and his teachers were in rapt attention.

"I know it was wrong, but I had fallen in love with Brön. He stayed a few more days and we spent every moment we could together. Eventually, he said he had to leave. The servants would start talking if he stayed any longer.

He promised to come back a few times per year to tend to the servants and to see to my welfare. I despaired after he left, more than once contemplating drowning myself in the river. Taking my own life was no more of a sin than adultery.

It occurred to me that he may have left me with child and so I waited a few weeks. When my courses did not come, hope blossomed within me as did our child.

He must have suspected as much because he came back about a week before the child was expected. Brön had changed. He looked healthy, fit, and seemed happier than he had when I last had seen him. He stayed to help with the delivery and left when my husband returned from his adventures. I had written to Sir Anthony with news of his impending fatherhood, and he had promised to return in time for the birth.

Brön had settled in Dublin and gave my husband his direction should we require further medical care. When Sir Anthony left two months later, I wrote to Brön, and he came at once."

SHE TURNED THEN to look at us, waiting for our judgment of her actions. Tom knew they were reprehensible in her time, but not so much in his own.

"Lady Callahan, I'd like to ask a very personal question," said Professor Ballantyne.

"After the tale I just old, I don't think there are many secrets between us."

"Yes. I appreciate the courage it took to share your story. What I would like to ask is if Brön fathered all of your children?"

Petunia looked deep into the fire before answering. She suddenly looked terribly sad and weary.

"I cannot be certain, but I would like to believe so," she said.

"Is he here now?" asked Professor Hilltop.

The tears were back, and she let them flow down her cheeks. Shaking her head she said, "He died saving our child."

CHAPTER
SIX

"WHAT HAPPENED?" asked Professor Ballantyne, searching her pockets for another handkerchief. When she found it, she went over to sit in the chair next to Petunia.

"He insisted on sleeping in the nursery with the children when he visited. Conor's birth had been difficult, and he was worried about the child's welfare.

One morning, I was shaken awake by Brady, my eldest, telling me to come to the nursery quickly. Ceased with dread, I ran from the bedroom.

When I arrived and saw Molly, the children's governess, weeping on the floor, I was sure something had happened to Conor. He was in Brön's arms, kicking up a fuss, while his father slept.

I ran to Ian's bed, and he was sound asleep and breathing normally. My children were fine. So why was Molly weeping instead of tending to Conor? The babe likely had a wet nappie. And how had Brön slept through all the commotion?

I plucked Conor from his arms and shook Brön's shoulder to wake him. I shouted his name and still, he would not wake."

Petunia paused, a fresh batch of tears rolling down her face.

"He was dead. I questioned Molly. The girl was hysterical and incoherent. I asked Brady if he knew what had happened. He said that Conor had been coughing or choking and that Brön had turned the baby over his arm and clapped his back. The couching had stopped and Brön rocked him back to sleep. Brady went back to bed and woke to Molly's screeching.

It didn't make sense. Brön may have been past his prime, but he was a hearty man. When Molly had calmed down, I asked her if there was more to Brady's story. She said that the baby's coughing had awoken her and that when she came to see him, the physician had things well in hand. As she was leaving the room to go back to bed, she said she saw Brön blessing the child and that a faint blue light seemed to be coming from his hand over the babe's head. She was afraid the physician was stealing the baby's soul, but when she woke and found him dead, she wondered if perhaps it had been the other way around.

I told her she was being ridiculous and asked her to fetch someone from downstairs to come for Brön's body. Seeing how she felt about Conor, you'll understand that she's been reassigned to other duties."

Petunia folded her hands on her lap, head bowed.

"I don't know what to make of it. I don't know if we were punished for our sins or if the curse kept him alive for all those years of Witch Hunting. He came back to life when we broke the curse, but perhaps his time was up. He was human, after all."

Tom and the others remained quiet, pausing to acknowledge the woman's grief over the man she loved.

Tom pondered his ancestor's tale. They had cleared up the mystery about the Witch Hunter's curse. It was plausible to assume the combination of a cursed Brön and a Witch would lead to a new breed of magic. If Brön had somehow transferred something to baby Conor before dying, it might explain how the new magical abilities had made their way to Tom. No one had said if the last known Blood Mage was one of Tom's ancestors.

There wasn't time to visit each of Conor's descendants. Mandy had waited long enough.

Tom's teachers must have come to the same conclusion because, after offering their sympathies and wishing Petunia well, they took their leave and returned to The Academy.

TOM AND PROFESSOR Hilltop were back at Harding with their report within minutes.

"If we had more time, I'm sure we could look into your lineage. As it is, I'm afraid we'll just have to assume that Conor is the source of the Blood Magick and that it was passed down selectively through the Callahan line," said Miss Clementine.

"I think we've waited long enough, it's time to get Mandy out of there," said Zaina, her jaw clenched, ready for battle.

They went over the plan one more time. Alistair was shuffling his feet, hands on his hips, and looking like he wanted to say something.

"Spit it out," said Tom.

The young man looked at Professor Montague and the Witch nodded her encouragement.

"What? What haven't you told me?" asked Tom, looking at everyone in the room in turn.

"The Master...you'll recognize him when you see him," Alistair said cryptically.

"What's that supposed to mean? Do I know him? Is it Professor Thunderbolt from The Academy? I swear the guy gives me the creeps," Tom said.

"No, Tom. While you were visiting Petunia, we looked at the brief memory I had of seeing his face. I can't be sure, as none of us have ever met him, but..."

"Who is it?!!?" screamed Tom.

"We think it's your father."

CHAPTER

SEVEN

ALISTAIR DIDN'T WAIT to gauge the impact of his truth bomb. He asked Lady Mathilda to open a Portal so he could return to The Master's lair before he was missed.

Tom was reeling. His father?? His father had been dead for over two years. Or had he. If his father was The Master, it explained a lot of unresolved bits of the puzzle, like why The Master has called him 'my son' or why he seemed intent on putting the house to rights after his minions had demolished the place, or even his obsession with Tom's ring.

What didn't compute was how a man as good and caring as his father could have turned into an evil Sorcerer intent on taking over the world. And if the Blood Magick was passed down from father to son, why had Tom inherited the power randomly on his sixteenth birthday?

If his father was The Master, how could they both have Blood Magick? Why didn't Tabitha have it, or Alistair for that matter?

"You'll hurt your brain, trying to figure it all out," said Zaina, placing a hand on his arm. "You've got this. "

"Zaina is right, Tom. Remember that even if The Master wears your father's face, it could be an illusion, or he could have used Blood

Magick to cure his illness. There's no telling the effect it might have had on him," explained Professor Hilltop.

"I don't mean to rush you, dear, but it's time," said Professor Montague gently.

"I've got this," said Tom, more to himself than anyone else, as he took out his Key. Professor Montague had written the coordinates to the castle on a piece of paper and Tom visualized the front door they'd seen.

"What about the wards?" he asked as his Door appeared.

"I'll come back to let you know when they're down," said Lady Mathilda.

She opened a Portal and, one by one, those assembled in Miss Clementine's office crossed over.

Tom paced the room as he waited. He debated whether to use the lancet to draw blood, just in case, but decided against it. He was smart and resourceful, if he'd learned anything these last few weeks. He could draw on his Traveler magic, on the spells he'd learned here at Harding, and on the knowledge he'd learned from books. And he can count on his friends and teachers to do their part.

I've got this.

Lady Mathilda's Portal appeared, and she poked her head out. "All clear!"

Tom nodded and she closed the Portal. She and the others would be posted around the castle while Tom drew The Master to the front.

Tom turned the handle and stepped out onto the dark gravel-lined drive leading up to the front door. The guards hadn't noticed him arriving; with the wards, Tom didn't think they were expecting company.

They did not hear him approach until he was a few feet from them. Tom raised his hands in surrender, ready to activate his shield if required.

"The Master is expecting me," he said simply. It was true enough since the Sorcerer had invited Tom to join him on more than one occasion.

The guards discussed it in low tones and one of them went in to validate Tom's claim.

After a few minutes, the guard came back and asked Tom to turn around. Once he had, the guard brought his arms down and tied them behind his back with a plastic zip tie.

A hood was placed on his head, and he was marched up the steps and into the castle.

They walked for quite a few minutes, turning this way and that, and Tom wondered if they were taking him in circles just to confuse him. He was only slightly worried that The Master wasn't intending on letting him leave once they'd had their conversation.

They finally stopped.

"Why is he bound and hooded?" asked The Master's distinct voice. Tom strained to hear any trace of his father, but all he heard was the raspy voice of an old mad man.

"It's procedure, Master," replied one of the guards, stammering a bit.

"For recruits, yes, not for our esteemed guest. Liberate him at once," he barked.

The hood came off and Tom blinked, his eyes adjusting to the pool of light he was in. There was a snap, and his hands were freed.

"Leave us," said The Master, dismissing his minions. Bathed as he was in light, the rest of the room was dark, and he could not immediately locate The Master until he spoke.

He was seated on a throne of sorts, on a dais about three feet off the ground. Getting his bearings, Tom saw the room was bare, though the walls held indistinguishable carvings.

The wall sconces were giving out a bit of light. Looking up, Tom saw he was under the room's only lit chandelier.

"Come closer, Tom. I won't bite," said The Master. He chuckled at his own attempt at humor.

Tom swallowed and moved forward, bracing himself for what lay ahead. He tried to remember that he should keep The Master talking for as long as he could so the others could get away.

The plan was for them to meet back at Harding. Once everyone was safe, Lady Mathilda would open a Portal to retrieve Tom if needed.

When Tom was only a few feet away from the dais, he looked up at the hooded figure.

"I believe you requested an audience with me?"

The Master chuckled again, a low rumble that echoed in the room.

"Don't worry, the girl is perfectly safe. The moleman was supposed to extend the invitation to you, but you can't blame him for making the mistake. Moles are notoriously nearsighted. No bother, it got you here, didn't it?"

"You might have sent a card and car to fetch me instead," replied Tom.

"As you were rather hostile in your refusal of my previous invitations, I felt I needed to get my point across somehow."

"Well, it worked. Here I am. What is it, exactly, that you need or want from me? And why me?" asked Tom.

The Master tented his fingers.

"The first question should be obvious. You are a Blood Mage. We are a rare breed," he said.

"So, you're one too?"

"Yes, I am. What I want and need from you requires a little more explanation," said The Master, drumming his fingers.

"I'm all ears and I have all night."

"At first, I wanted to make sure you were the one. I've tested so many of your kin. There was even one very promising prospect, a cousin of sorts, but though he is a talented Warlock, he has no Blood Magick."

It was on the tip of Tom's tongue to ask if he was referring to Alistair, but as they weren't supposed to have met yet, Tom kept his mouth shut and his face neutral.

CHAPTER

EIGHT

THE GROUP EXITED the Portal just outside the wall near the side entrance Arturo had identified as the one closest to Mandy. Lady Mathilda remained on stand-by.

Professors Montague, Hilltop, and Bellamy got to work on the wards. They spread out about three feet apart and extended their arms in the air as though holding a giant medicine ball.

"Can we help?" asked Benny. "I don't know anything about taking down magical wards, but isn't this one of those instances where the more Witches and Warlocks, the better?"

"It is, but I'd prefer you three keep up your strength and focus for what comes next. While you go in, we'll hold down the fort out here," said Professor Montague turning back to focus on the wards.

The three teachers were chanting the same three words in Latin over and over, '*confractus, continentia, emissio*', which loosely translated into 'break, containment, release'.

Soon, Arturo, Zaina, and Benny could see the shimmer of the wards. It was working. The air above the wall became a smoky white that slowly vanished with the wards. They were in.

Well, almost. They needed to find a way through the thick stone wall. A door or gate would be best. They could blast their way through, of course, but they would lose the element of surprise.

Arturo rose above the wall and looked to either side of their position for an opening. He spotted a gate about fifteen feet to their left. The rescue party trekked through the woods to the gate, and Zaina did the honor of unlocking it.

While Tom and the Professors had been Time Walking, Zaina had gone to the armory to retrieve a few artifacts that might come in handy. She had golden ropes, death marbles, and a magic carpet stuffed into her backpack. She also had a wand, which she never used, and a pouch of fairy magic dust, which she could use to temporarily blind her attackers.

She cracked her knuckles and said, "Let's do this."

Everyone agreed that Professor Bellamy went first. Hunched over and sporting a walking stick, she moved slowly toward the side door. It took a while for anyone to notice the elderly Witch and when they did, the guards ambled her way. Once they were close enough, she asked them to help her sit down so she could rest her tired old legs. When they each took an arm to help her along, she grabbed their hands and subjected them to the illusion she had selected beforehand. It was a memory of a safari she had taken in Africa.

Next was Zaina. She sauntered past the guards, whistling loudly, hoping to catch the attention of the guards on the roof. Sure enough, they spotted her and yelled down to the immobile guards. They couldn't hear anything but the sounds of an approaching ostrich stampede. They started running toward the stone wall, with Professor Bellamy struggling to keep up.

Before they could hit the wall and hurt themselves, Professor Montague hit them with a sleeping spell, and they crumbled to the ground.

"Thank you, dear, I haven't run in over fifty years. I need to catch my breath," she said, panting.

"You've done well, have a rest. We'll take it from here," said Professor Hilltop, guiding his colleague to a rock on the other side of the wall next to Benny and Arturo

Spotting the guards on the roof, he aimed a stunning spell at each of them. One of them fell back onto the roof, but the other lost balance and fell into the open. Professor Hilltop waved his wand and the Warlock floated down, light as a feather, and lay sleeping on the gravel.

It was Arturo and Benny's turn. They walked to where Zaina was, keeping an eye on the door in case the guards were missed and more came to take their place. Arturo waved goodbye and rose off the ground until he was between the two upper windows. He moved sideways to peek into the first window. The room appeared empty. He moved to the other window and saw Mandy, still bound and gagged in her chair, eyes closed. The rest of the room also looked empty.

Arturo tapped the glass gently, hoping to get her attention. Mandy immediately opened her eyes and turned to look at the window. Her surprised expression quickly turned to excitement, though she kept turning and nodding her head toward the door.

Arturo put up a hand and mouthed 'it's ok' before looking down at Zaina and Benny to give them a thumbs up.

He tried to lift the window, but it was locked or painted shut. *Nothing a little magic couldn't fix*, he thought. Since he needed most of his concentration to maintain his hovering position, he used a transfiguration spell to turn the window glass into vapor so he could slip inside.

Arturo went in and patted Mandy, holding a finger to his lips so Mandy would remain quiet. He removed the gag, then untied her hands and feet. Mandy jumped up and threw her arms around his neck, holding on for dear life. Stunned, Arturo awkwardly patted her back and whispered in her ear.

"Zaina and Benny are on their way from the inside. When it's safe to leave, they will open the door."

Mandy nodded her understanding and slowly peeled herself off Arturo, giving him an embarrassed smile. He nodded for her to follow him, and they went to stand against the wall by the door, like two FBI agents about to burst through.

CHAPTER
NINE

ARTURO HAD GIVEN them the all-clear. Zaina took the lead and Benny followed close behind.

The door wasn't locked, and Zaina hugged the doorway, letting only her head pass the threshold to make sure the coast was clear.

They slipped inside and closed the door soundlessly. They padded down the hallway stopping before every door and hugging the walls to ensure no minions lurked. Though they were ready for a fight, they weren't looking to engage the enemy if they didn't have to. This was a rescue mission, not an attack.

They finally made it to the stairs and Zaina motioned for Benny to take the lead; she would cover him. Benny kept both hands up, ready to freeze anyone that came his way. Meanwhile, Zaina was taking the stairs backward, her wand trained on the first floor.

So far, so good.

They made it to the landing without issue. Benny paused to wait for Zaina. He pointed left, then right; he couldn't remember which way to go. Zaina indicated it was to the right and he started down the hallway as she followed, again walking backward to get the jump on anyone who might exit one of the many rooms.

They had expected guards to be posted outside Mandy's door, but there were no Warlocks to be seen. There were three doors with rooms facing the courtyard they'd come in from. They would have to check each one.

Hugging the wall, Zaina knocked on the door softly and waited. "Arturo!" she whispered, but there was no response. She motioned for Benny to try the next door. He moved passed her and knocked on the door. "Mandy?" he whispered.

He heard a soft "Benny!" in response and turned to Zaina to let her know he'd found the right door. He tried the handle, but it was locked. Zaina walked over, aimed her wand at it, and unlocked the door.

"I'm so happy to see you!" exclaimed Mandy.

"Shhh!" replied Zaina, grabbing Mandy and giving Arturo a tactical signal meaning she'd cover Mandy, and he should cover Benny.

They retraced their steps down the hall and down the steps. The group was steps away from the door when they heard a sound so chilling that they stopped dead in their tracks. It was the sound of a loaded shotgun.

"Don't move. Slowly put your hands behind your head and kneel on the floor. If one of you tries to be a hero, you all die," said the voice.

Arturo, Benny, Mandy, and Zaina complied and slowly sank to the ground. When Zaina tried to look around, the voice barked, "Don't turn around."

Someone came and tied their hands with zip ties and placed hoods over their heads.

"We should gag them so they can't yell curses at us," another voice called from behind them.

"Good point, get some rags from the kitchen," the main voice said.

As the minion hurried away, the Warlock spoke to them.

"Did you really think you could walk out of here as easy as that? When the guards didn't check-in, we looked at the monitors and saw you coming. We figured it was easier to let you get your friend here and catch you on your way out."

They heard footsteps as the minion returned with the rags. He tied them over the hoods, which made it difficult to breathe.

The minion helped each of them stand up, turned them in the

direction they would be walking, and made sure they each felt the butt of the rifle at the small of their backs.

"Let's go meet The Master," said the faceless voice.

CHAPTER
TEN

THE MASTER PAUSED and seemed to be gauging Tom's reaction. He pursed his lips and continued with his explanation.

"Now that we've established that you are the next Blood Mage, we can begin," he said.

Tom's neutral facade cracked. "The *next* Blood Mage?"

"Yes. There can only be one true Blood Mage at a time."

Tom frowned.

This makes no sense. He just said he was a Blood Mage too.

The Master shifted on his throne as though happy to have elicited a reaction from Tom.

"I can see you are confused. Think of it as a nobility title. A Duke, for example, will pass on the Dukedom to his heir. If he does not produce an heir, the title will pass to the next male in the line of succession."

Tom nodded.

"Does that mean you and I are related?" he asked as casually as he could. Tom was desperately trying to keep his composure, but he was tired of remaining on the cusp of the matter.

"Yes, of course, we are related!" exclaimed The Master. In his exuberance, Tom thought he heard the faintest of Irish accents.

Tom waited with bated breath, dying to ask how they were related. He had no idea how much time had passed since he'd arrived and if it had been enough time for the others to extract Mandy.

It was best to stall as long as he could. He was in no immediate danger, and he wanted to hear the tale.

"Are you my grandfather?"

The Master bowed and chuckled. His response was cryptic.

"I am the grandfather of Blood Magick."

Right. Now what?

Tom wondered if an alarm would go off when Mandy was discovered missing or if one had already sounded when the wards were breached. For all Tom knew, The Master could be stalling *him*.

"Am I to assume that you have to die for me to inherit the title of Blood Mage?"

It was a bold question, but Tom was sure it wouldn't anger the old Sorcerer. If anything, he'd be proud of Tom for showing some backbone.

"The simple answer is yes," said The Master, rising from his throne. Tom tried to catch a glimpse of his face as he paced slowly on the dais. But he was too far away from the light and all Tom could see was the pasty whiteness of his skin.

"What's the complicated answer?" asked Tom. When The Master paused but did not reply, Tom added, "Does it have anything to do with Petunia Eva?"

The Master's head shot up and he turned to look at Tom. "What do you know about Petunia?"

"I've met her. Twice. She had a lot to say," replied Tom. He could be cryptic too.

"Tell me, boy!"

"If I do, will you tell me who you are? How we are related, and what needs to happen for the madness to stop?"

Tom cringed inwardly. He hoped The Master didn't think Tom was calling *him* mad. It was never good to tell crazy people that they were crazy.

"Yes, of course. That's why you're here, isn't it?"

Tom nodded and gave The Master the cliff notes version of his visits with Petunia.

The Master had resumed his position on the throne. He listened attentively, hands tented again, and did not interrupt. When Tom was done, all The Master said was that he wished he could Travel through Doors.

"If we're related, wouldn't you also have the Traveling gene?"

The Master nodded, or at least that's what it looked like to Tom.

"As I'm sure you are aware, Petunia's son, Conor, had twin sons, one of which is your ancestor. Larkin married a Traveler named Sara. In Traveling families, succession is very much like nobility titles in the sense that the heir, or Custodian, must marry and produce at least two children. For some reason, Travelers usually have two children, a boy and a girl. Traditionally, the boy was chosen as heir and Custodian, regardless of whether he was the eldest or not. In more recent times, the eldest is selected. But they have the option of passing on the duties to their sibling, if the sibling is willing. Is that not how you became Custodian?"

"Yes, it is," replied Tom, not bothering to ask how The Master knew this.

"What you may not realize is that the sibling who is not the Custodian will not pass on the gene to their children unless they marry a Traveler who is Custodian for *their* family. For example, your sister Tabitha will retain the use of her Key for as long as she lives and, under the rules of Traveler succession, may also reside at the family home for as long as she chooses. But unless she marries a Custodian, any children she may bear will not be Travelers."

Tom hadn't thought about it before. He knew a lot of Travelers married within their circle, but he had assumed that was from some antiquated notion to maintain or increase wealth. If Tom hadn't taken over as Custodian, the line would have died with him. Even if he and Lola married, their children wouldn't have been Travelers because her brother Devlin was Custodian, not her.

Thinking of Lola gave Tom a sinking feeling. The last time he'd seen her, he thought they were making in-roads on the way to reconciliation. He hadn't had a chance to update her since he visited her Sunday. What if he never saw her again? There was a chance he could die tonight.

Tom shook the thought away. It was crazy talk, and he didn't have time for that now. Returning his focus to the conversation, he tried to understand how the information The Master had just shared had any bearing on their current situation.

"What does that have to do with you not having a Traveling gene. Are you the son of a non-Custodian?"

"Something like that," said The Master.

Tom reminded himself that he was supposed to stretch this out as long as possible, until Lady Mathilda confirmed that everyone was safely back at Harding Academy. Nonetheless, the pace at which The Master was doling out information was maddening. It was like he was a bird being fed tiny morsels of chewed-up food by its mother.

I wish he'd get on with it.

The Master rose again. This time he paced on the other side of the throne.

"Blood Magick isn't a gene like Traveling. You could say it's more like a mutation. Anyone from a human magical bloodline has the predisposition," he began as though he was in a lecture hall filled with fascinated attendees.

As an audience of one, Tom was in rapt. *We're getting somewhere now. He makes it sound like a virus or an inheritable disease.*

Tom took in The Master's slightly hunched posture, chalk-white face, and bony fingers and concluded he wasn't far off.

However, before The Master could continue, there was a knock on the door at the other end of the ballroom. Tom jumped and turned to look at the door.

CHAPTER

ELEVEN

"WHAT DO YOU WANT?" he said in the voice he'd used on Tom during their showdown at the house. He'd spoken barely above a whisper, yet Tom had heard him as clearly as if he'd been standing right behind him.

Gooseflesh spread over Tom's arms, and he could only imagine how the knocker felt for interrupting.

The door opened a crack and a hooded head poked in.

"Pardon me, Master. There's been a development I think you should be made aware of."

Tom turned back to The Master to see how he would respond.

"Do tell," replied The Master, his voice dripping with sarcasm as it echoed around the room.

Even Tom knew that this interruption better be important. He hoped it was for the minion's sake. Tom didn't feel like witnessing a murder.

His gaze went back to the Warlock. He stood in the middle of the room, much like Tom was. It felt like he was watching a Wimbledon match; winner takes all.

"We've apprehended some intruders, Master. They came for the girl, just like you said they would."

Tom blanched. The Master had anticipated this. How stupid to have thought they could get away with it. Truthfully, Tom assumed he'd taken Mandy to get his attention and that he would relinquish her once he had Tom in his grasp.

"More guests!" said The Master with excitement. "Do show them in!"

The Warlock bowed his head in obvious relief and waved to whoever waited in the hall. The double doors opened, and four figures were ushered into the ballroom.

"Are these the teachers or the children?" asked The Master.

It was hard to tell with the black sacks on their heads. Since they all were dressed in black robes, Tom had a look at their feet. He spotted Zaina's hi-tops and didn't know whether to be relieved or worried. This hadn't been the plan. Getting caught put his friends in danger. Then again, maybe he could barter for all of them the way he'd prepared to for Mandy.

"It's the kids, Master. I'm sure they had help, but we couldn't find anyone else on the property."

"I see. And why did you feel the need to contain them in such an ungracious manner?"

The Master was back on his throne, waving a dismissive hand at the new arrivals. His words were low and raspy, and seemed to bounce off the walls and creep up from every direction as though he wore a microphone plugged into a surround sound system.

"The girl kept trying to freeze us with her magic, so we had to tie her hands. Then she tried to curse us, so we gagged her. When this lot showed up, we didn't take any chances."

"Quite right," said The Master, and the minion seemed to preen a little.

"Bring them to the center of the room so I can get a closer look at them."

The Warlock and his helper guided their charges to stand under the chandelier.

"Fetch some chairs for all of them and remove the sacks from their heads. It wouldn't do to have them die of asphyxiation," ordered The Master and the Warlock hopped to it.

They brought a chair for Tom too, and he felt a little ridiculous sitting on a chair in the middle of the room. One by one, the gags and sacks were removed, and his friends gulped in air. Upon seeing Tom, they looked relieved to see him, though Benny mouthed the words 'I'm sorry' to Tom with a dismal shrug. The Warlocks unbound their hands and secured them to the chairs.

Once they were done, the Warlocks looked to The Master for further instructions.

"You may go. I can handle a few teenagers on my own," he said.

The Warlocks bowed and left the room.

It had been a good plan. But it was time for plan B.

"Please let them go," said Tom. "It's me you wanted; you don't need them."

"You're right. I don't need them, but they make excellent leverage."

"Why do you need leverage? I said I would stay and see this through," said Tom, getting up now. He didn't feel powerful sitting on a dining room chair.

"Indeed, you did. However, once you hear what I have to say, you may very well change your mind. This way, I know you'll stay put to keep your friends safe. Meanwhile, they'll behave because they want to keep you safe. It's a win-win situation. For me, anyway," replied The Master. "Besides, it's much more enjoyable telling a story to a crowd than to a single person."

When Tom remained standing, hands on his hips in defiance, The Master added, "Have a seat, Tom. It's a long tale, and I promise not to lay a finger on any of you. At least not until the end of my story."

Tom stared at The Master for a beat. There was no reason to trust him, but then again, there wasn't much Tom could do. Sure, he could awaken his Blood Magick and attack, but he knew The Master was about to reveal essential information to solve this puzzle.

He turned to look at his friends. Zaina shrugged, Arturo nodded, Mandy shot daggers at The Master, and Benny started to cry soundlessly.

Tom took a deep breath and sat down. It was story time.

CHAPTER

TWELVE

PROFESSORS BELLAMY, Montague, and Hilltop huddled in the woods outside the castle walls, anxiously waiting for the students to come out. They had neutralized the outer guards easily enough. At present, they were sleeping peacefully in the rotunda on the other side of the castle, except for the one who was asleep on the roof and the other who'd fallen off the roof. It had been easier to simply pull him behind some shrubberies.

The others had simply followed Professor Hilltop. Using a transfiguration spell, he had taken on the appearance of one of the sleeping Warlocks and exclaimed that the western wall had been breached.

Eyes trained on the door, they waited.

"It's taking too long," worried Professor Bellamy.

"I'm sure they're just being cautious and taking their time," replied Professor Hilltop.

"I wonder how Tom is making out. Should someone pop in and have a look while we wait?" asked Professor Montague.

"You're not seriously going to sit on the damp earth with Warlocks lurking about to astral project are you?" asked Professor Bellamy, placing a concerned hand on her colleague's wrist.

"No, of course not. I'll just lean against this tree and close my eyes, if you watch over me while I'm away from my body," she replied.

"I'll watch you and Hilda can watch for the children," said Professor Hilltop, following Professor Montague to the tree she had selected.

It took less than a minute and she was out. Walking through the wall, she crossed the courtyard and entered the castle. Things were ever quiet, too quiet. She went up the stairs, toward the room where they were keeping Mandy. She found it empty.

Perplexed, she checked each of the upper rooms. The students were nowhere to be found.

She went back to the first floor and checked the rooms there too. She wondered if Lady Mathilda had already come for them.

She followed the hall leading to the front of the house, listening for signs of life. As she went further into the castle, she started picking up clinking sounds. Sure enough, she found a handful of Warlocks having a late-night snack in the kitchen.

She entered the kitchen to listen in on their conversation, hoping to pick up some useful information.

"I can't believe you had the guts to knock on the door!" one of the Warlocks was saying.

Professor Montague thought they didn't look so menacing with their hoods off. They were barely older than Tom and his friends. Professor Montague wondered what had happened to Jameson. He wasn't in the kitchen. Was he outside sleeping in the rotunda with the other bewitched guards?

No, Jameson was clever. He'd be higher up than a mere guard if there were ranks among The Master's minions. His acolytes, however, were not.

She peered at each face but didn't recognize any of them as the students who had been expelled from Harding Academy. More to the point, Alistair wasn't with them, nor had he been among those they had neutralized.

When the boy said he had to get back or he would be missed, they had thought he meant back to the castle. But it was entirely possible that he was on a mission for the Magical Foreign Office. It was evening in the UK, but he could be working in another part of the world.

Intent as she was on her musings, she didn't want to miss something one of them said.

"I don't know what he wants with those other Witches and Warlocks. I hope he doesn't plan on asking them to join us. That Arturo fellow is such a know-it-all."

"Oh, yeah. I remember him. He was the one who could levitate. I guess that's how they got in," the other replied.

Professor Montague had heard enough. She left the kitchen and continued down the hall, going from room to room until she finally found her quarry.

They were seated in a half-circle in the middle of the room, facing the Warlock on the throne. The Master. She didn't dare enter the room completely. Some Warlocks could feel the energy shift when someone was visiting from beyond and she didn't want to lose the advantage of being hidden from sight.

As far as she could tell, the children were unharmed. Though four of them had their hands tied behind their backs. All of them but Benny actively tried to loosen the ropes as discreetly as possible.

The children were listening to The Master. She might have lingered to hear what he was saying but she needed to get back to her body. She retreated to the hall, crossed into an adjoining room, and flew out into the night air.

She hovered above her body for a moment. Professor Hilltop was keeping watch, as promised, while Professor Bellamy was staring owl-eyed at the side door. She slipped into her body and opened her eyes.

"I'm afraid I have bad news."

CHAPTER
THIRTEEN

"NOW, WHERE WAS I?" asked The Master.

When it appeared like he was actually waiting for an answer, Tom cleared his throat and said, "You had just said that Blood Magick was a mutation that can affect anyone from a magical bloodline."

"Dear boy, you make it sound like a degenerative disease!" said The Master, clearly appalled.

Isn't it?

"It is a gift that chooses its recipient from among the current host's progeny."

Host?

Tom chanced a sidelong look at Zaina. Her brows were furrowed. Yeah, she'd caught that too.

"I'm not sure I understand. Now it sounds like an alien invasion," said Tom. He wasn't trying to antagonize The Master, but he thought going the direct route might speed things along. It was getting late, and it had already been a long day. He needed to stay sharp.

The Master burst out laughing. It was more of a rumbling cackle, really.

"Tom, you're being cheeky, and I like it!" He rose with more vigor as though Tom's verbal sparring had given him energy. Instead of pacing on the dais as he had before, he levitated off the dais and came to stand a few feet in front of his audience. Hands behind his back, he resumed his tale as though it was an inspiring TED Talk.

"Although most magical humans can physically receive the gift, direct descendants are always the ideal recipients. Their body chemistry closely matches the Blood Mage's and that increases the likelihood of success."

"You're saying it sometimes fails?" asked Tom. He was thoroughly creeped out now.

"Sadly, yes. Some people cannot handle the power. If it's not taken back immediately, they die," The Master said gravely.

Seeing Tom's horrified expression mirrored on his friends' faces, he hurried to add, "But not you, Tom. You're strong. You've already demonstrated yourself to be more than up to the task. In fact, I'd wager there's never been a better candidate. Perhaps it's because you inherited a little more magic or because your father died before he could receive the gift."

"My father? He wasn't a Blood Mage, then?" asked Tom.

As excited as Tom might have been to see his father again, he had to admit he was a little relieved. When Tom had learned that one of the Blood Magick abilities was Necromancy, a terrible thought had lodged itself at the back of Tom's mind. What if The Master had brought someone back to life after they died? It was preposterous. Why would someone do that... unless they cared for the person and didn't want to let go. Like their child, their spouse, or their parent. Or if the person had asked them to do it before they died...

"He should have been, but his illness made him too weak," replied The Master.

"Wait. Are you saying *that's* what killed him? You tried to give him the 'gift' and he couldn't handle the power and he died??"

Tom felt dizzy and nauseous. For years, he had no one to blame for his father's death; Nowhere to direct his pain, his rage, and his sorrow. Cancer was an unconquerable enemy. Tom's blood started to boil, and the air around him crackled like the heat coming off his body was popping invisible kernels of corn.

"Be chill," said Zaina under her breath. "You don't want to start world war three."

She was right. He had to keep his wits about him. Tom tamped down on the anger, pushing it until it was a low simmer.

"I'm afraid so. You have to understand, we both thought it would cure him," said The Master.

"You killed my father," said Tom flatly. He was beyond angry now. He'd detached from his feelings and was merely stating a fact.

"I killed my son!" screamed The Master, flying toward Tom and stopping within an inch of his face.

CHAPTER
FOURTEEN

ALISTAIR FELT bad for his cousin. He wished he could do more to help Tom. As it was, he'd nearly blown his cover when he returned to the castle. He had sent word to the CEMB that he would be alone in his office at The Master's castle around eight p.m.

The Brothers, as The Master's minions were called, knew not to disturb Allistair when his office door was closed. And there were no windows looking out into the castle's library, so no one could peer into his office to spy.

Half-a-dozen Brothers were assigned to library duty, under Alistair's command, and their work usually concluded at six. Most went home to their families, but a few lived too far to commute every day and stayed in rooms on the third floor

Alistair lived at the castle too. When the MFO had called him back from a job in Italy to infiltrate The Master's organization, Alistair had agreed immediately.

So far, they'd given him tame, pencil-pushing assignments in corporate settings. When he was hired by the MFO a year ago, he had been dreaming of Bond-worthy missions. The truth was that he was neither in the secret service nor was he a spy. Nonetheless, he had worked diligently, used his time-slowing power to observe more closely than most agents could, and sent detailed, comprehensive reports in the hopes that he would catch someone's eye at the MFO.

And catch someone's eye he did, but not for his mad skills and experience. They had selected him because of his Callahan name; his skills were a pleasant bonus.

He had been briefed by the MFO and the CEMB. He would have liked to interview the prisoners at The Hold himself, but it was too risky. Not because there was any danger, but because word might get out and blow his cover. Instead, he'd read boxes and boxes of files and notes on the ongoing investigation.

The trail started a year ago when a Traveler named Phyllis Evers had been kidnapped while shopping in Italy. At the time, the CEMB had ruled it accidental and let the Traveler's Council deal with it.

However, a few weeks later, the same perpetrator was involved in the attempted kidnapping of Miss Evers' niece and nephew, Lola and Devlin Evers.

As the plot unraveled, four people were arrested, tried, and sent to The Hold for their part in an elaborate scheme to secure Traveling magical artifacts such as Keys, Time Watches, and Spheres.

The CEMB wouldn't have interfered if the culprits had merely stolen family heirlooms. But since these items also enabled them to Travel anywhere, including the past, the future, and any known world, swift and immediate action was required.

In addition, the CEMB reached out to all Traveling families to strongly suggest that they store their artifacts at the CEMB's secure headquarters. Also, to inform them that Time Walking and World Jumping would be restricted and legislated activities henceforth. Most families complied without complaint if only to avoid being burglarized again.

As the culprits had also used the items to separate wealthy non-magical humans from their money, they were also charged with dangerous exposure. Their stay at The Hold would be extensive.

Meanwhile, the Brother and The Master, deemed responsible, were still at large. Though they couldn't be certain, the CEMB believed that the Brother in question was the Warlock who had died at the hands of Tom Callahan. The incident had been ruled an accident, especially since Tom was a minor attending The Academy.

The deceased Warlock was Shaun Murphy. He had been a close friend of the late John Callahan, Tom's father. Alistair had gone to school with Derek, Shaun's son, and would have attended the wake even if the CEMB hadn't asked. The wake was in Alistair's own Parish in Derrymore, just west of Belfast.

He and Derek hadn't kept in touch after Uni, but they'd been friends while at school. Derek was brilliant at potions and had been studying Applied Biochemistry. He'd graduated with honors and gone on to work at a top Biochem company in Germany.

The CEMB tasked Alistair with renewing his friendship with Derek in the hopes that the son might be approached by The Master to take over for his father and, with any luck, Alistair might also be recruited.

As luck would have it, Derek was already being recruited by The Master. When Alistair expressed utter dissatisfaction with his current position, citing how boring and tedious it was, Derek had started slowly dropping hints about the freelance work he was doing for a new employer here in the UK.

Alistair was playing the long game, so he didn't react to the first few hints. As they were both staying in their parents' homes at the moment, they'd been meeting regularly to catch up, go on hikes, or grab a beer at the pub.

When Derek mentioned that he'd be going to Scotland to visit his employer's facility, Alistair kicked things up a notch.

"It's near the coast in northern Scotland," explained Derek. "The exact location is confidential."

"How will you get there?" asked Alistair.

"I was provided with an address and was told a car would pick me up and take me to the facility. Free room and board are provided not only during the visit but for any employee hired full-time. It's in a castle!"

"Sounds amazing. I wonder if they might have a job for me, but I'm not a scientist," replied Alistair.

Derek perked up at Alistair's first clear sign of interest.

"I've actually spoken of you to my contact. I hope you don't mind, but he was very interested. It seems they are looking for someone young and fresh to join their corporate relations team."

Alistair's beaming smile was genuine. First, he was in. Second, if this hadn't been an undercover assignment, the job offer would have been very exciting for someone his age.

"That sounds incredible. Do you think I could go with you to visit the place? Could they interview me at the same time?"

"That's precisely what my contact suggested. You'll need to send him your resume and he'll want to conduct a phone interview," explained Derek.

"Yes, of course. Anything!"

Derek had given him a business card. "You can keep it; I have another at home."

It looked authentic. There was a corporate logo for a company called Vardo Ventures. Their headquarters were based in Oslo, Norway. Alistair checked their website, it too seemed genuine. He relayed the information to the CEMB and sent his resume to Mr. Edgar Nielsen, director of Human Resources.

Within an hour, Mr. Nielsen sent his reply, inviting Alistair to a phone interview later that day, if he was available. As it happened, he was.

The interview went well. Mr. Nielsen asked typical questions regarding Alistair's current position, which had been fabricated to avoid linking him to the MFO. He explained the role and asked about Alistair's goals and ambitions.

The recruiter seemed satisfied with Alistair's answers because he invited him to a second interview and to tour the facility with Derek. Alistair quickly accepted. Before ending the interview, Mr. Nielsen explained that per the company's health and safety policy, all employees must consent to the drug and alcohol testing protocol.

"You mean like a blood and urine test?" asked Alistair.

"Yes. New hires undergo mandatory testing before starting. Further testing is done randomly every six months."

"I understand. It's the same at my current job."

"Very well. I'll email you the itinerary and instructions later this afternoon. As I will not be in attendance, I'll be reaching out to you in a few days to see how it went."

"Thank you, Sir. I look forward to it," replied Alistair.

CHAPTER
FIFTEEN

THE FLIGHT from Belfast to Aberdeen was a little over an hour. As neither Alistair nor Derek had ever visited this part of Scotland, they had arrived a few days before to take in the sights.

Once settled at their hotel, they rented a car and drove up the coast to visit a few castles and other interesting landmarks. They concluded their visit with a tour of the city and dinner at one of the posher restaurants in town.

The next morning, they packed a lunch and headed for Cairngorms National Park. The park didn't have any challenging hikes, but it was beautiful, and they managed to hit a good many trails before calling it a day at dusk. They stopped at a roadside pub for dinner, returned the car, and went to bed early.

After breakfast, they checked out of the hotel and waited for the car that Vardo Ventures would be sending.

It wasn't a limousine; it was a sleek black car with tinted windows, the make of which Alistair didn't know. The driver placed their luggage in the trunk and opened the door to the back seat for them.

The windows were opaque, and the only light was coming from the front seat.

Once the driver was behind the wheel, he turned back to his passengers.

"The windows are tinted so you won't see where we're going. It's a forty-five-minute drive to our destination. Help yourself to some refreshments," he said, pointing at a basket on the floor. "When we arrive, don't be alarmed. You'll be blindfolded and taken to a secure room to meet with someone from HR. It's just a precaution. We've had issues with corporate espionage in the past, I'm afraid. Any questions before we set off?"

Derek looked uneasily at Alistair. He clearly hadn't been expecting this level of cloak and dagger. To put him at ease, Alistair said, "Sure, mate. We understand. I was once blindfolded to attend a meeting on another floor at my other job. It's unnerving, but not as uncommon as people might think."

Satisfied, the driver nodded, turned on the lights in the backseat, and activated the partition between them. Once it was up, Derek and Alistair were basically in a moving black box.

Since Derek still looked a little worried, Alistair smiled and rubbed his hands. "What's in the basket, do you think?"

As they explored the contents, Alistair spoke about their years at Uni together. Soon, Derek relaxed, and they spent the ride reminiscing about easier days.

The car slowed and came to a stop. The partition came down and the driver gave them each a large silk blindfold and asked them to put it on. They were in front of some sort of gate. As it was solid metal, it was impossible to make out where they were.

Once they'd donned what was essentially a fancy sleep mask, the driver closed the partition and put the car into gear.

"GENTLEMEN, welcome! I apologize for the theatrics. Our facility is home to highly sensitive technology, and we take our privacy very seriously," said the elegantly dressed young woman that had entered the room they were waiting in.

They nodded.

"Mr. Murphy, if you'll come with me, I'll take you to meet Dr. Müeller."

Derek rose and followed her to the door.

"Mr. Callahan, Mrs. Morgenthaler will be with you shortly," she said before they left.

"Thank you."

Alistair rose from his chair. Aware that he may be under surveillance, he made it appear that he was merely stretching his legs after a long car ride, shaking them out, rolling his shoulders. To the casual observer, he looked like a young man trying to relax before an important interview.

He got a quick glance out the window but didn't see much. The window was fogged up and he could only catch what looked like a small walled-in garden.

The door opened and Mrs. Morgenthaler came in.

"Hello, Mr. Callahan. I'm Mrs. Morgenthaler, head of HR for this facility," she said, extending a hand.

Alistair shook it firmly, and replied, "Pleased to meet you. Thank you for inviting me."

"You're most welcome. If you'll follow me, we'll conduct the interview in another room."

Alistair followed her out into the hall. They stopped about three doors down and entered a plain-looking boardroom. Two men and one woman were seated at the table. They smiled briefly and Alistair made eye contact with each of them before taking the seat that was offered.

Mrs. Morgenthaler went over the non-disclosure agreement that was in front of him. Once he had signed, the other attendees were introduced, and the interview began.

Alistair assumed everyone in the room was a Witch or Warlock, but he couldn't be sure. It was a completely routine interview for the role he was applying for. When he asked what product or services Vardo

Ventures offered, he was provided with a vague outline and told more would be revealed at the next step of the hiring process.

If he'd been interviewing for this position, he'd have enough information to decide whether to continue or not.

"At present, we would like to go forward. If you do not, the car will take you back to your hotel in Aberdeen," said Mrs. Morgenthaler at the end of the interview.

"I'd like to go forward," replied Alistair. His curiosity was peaked, and his mission was moving along.

The head of HR smiled and gestured to the door, "We've arranged for you to have lunch with prospective colleagues so you can ask questions in an informal setting. We'll meet back here in an hour."

Alistair thanked her and everyone at the table and turned to the door where a young man waited.

"Hi, I'm Nathan. I'm a corporate lawyer here at Vardo Ventures," he said, extending his hand. Alistair shook it. The guy was about his age, perhaps a year or two older. "Come on, I'll show you to the executive dining room."

CHAPTER
SIXTEEN

THE DINING ROOM WAS FULL. Well-dressed employees were seated at banquet-style tables of six. Nathan led the way to a remote section with only two tables. Alistair saw Derek at one of the tables, talking animatedly with three others. He looked up at Alistair as he neared and beamed.

Alistair gave him a thumbs up and sat at the other table. He was introduced to Maria, Helmut, and Josette. They had a lovely lunch and Alistair wished he could work here with these very cool people.

While they did not disclose any confidential information, they were able to shed light on the day-to-day operations, the company culture, the benefits, and life at the castle for those who chose to live there.

When their time was up, Alistair felt as though he'd made new friends. There was no talk of magic, and he wondered again whether his potential colleagues were regular humans or not.

He walked back to the boardwalk with Nathan. "I hope to see you again," the young man offered. "I don't live here, so I won't know if you stayed until tomorrow. But Helmut and Josette will see you at dinner, should you choose to stay for the next round."

They shook hands. Alistair smiled and took his seat. It was only Mrs. Morgenthaler in the boardroom. She asked if he wished to continue the hiring process and he agreed. She went over the consent form for the Drug and Alcohol testing Protocol as well as a form for cognitive, personality, and biometric testing.

Although he didn't relish the idea of having blood drawn, he was excited about the other tests. He enjoyed the pre-employment tests, and he often did very well. He signed the consent forms.

"The cognitive and personality tests will be done on the computer," she explained, placing a laptop in front of Alistair. You'll have one hour to complete each test with a short break between the two. Do you need to use the lavatory before you begin?"

Alistair didn't need the toilet, but he said he did, and he was shown to a small powder room a few doors down. Once inside, he used a spell to locate cameras or other listening devices. There were none. He took out his mobile, input his scrambling code, and sent a text to his liaison at the MFO.

If they took his phone, they would see he'd written to his mother to let her know he'd passed the first stages of the interview and was now about to do a personality assessment. His "mam" sent back a thumb emoji and he smiled.

He used the toilet, washed his hands, and exited the powder room.

It took him thirty-eight minutes to complete the cognitive assessment, and forty-two minutes to complete the employee personality profile. Next, he was given an Inbox Simulation. The online test recreates the traditional inbox/outbox exercise to measure core managerial skills.

Next, his listening, reading, writing, speaking, and problem-solving skills were tested. Six scenarios were presented in different formats. A printed complaint letter from a dissatisfied vendor, a voice message from a disgruntled employee, a video message from a superior who expressed concerns about his performance, and four emails from co-workers from various departments. He needed to assess each one, determine the best course of action, and respond through the same media that the original message was sent.

This task took the longest and he hadn't been given a deadline, though he was aware he was being timed. He had them sorted in under an hour. He had expected to simply write his letter, send the emails, and record responses to the voice and video message.

However, a phone was provided to respond to the voicemail. When he picked up the receiver, he was surprised to find a live person at the other end of the line. Alistair thought he handled the call well.

For the video message response, there was an actual video conference where he interacted with one of the men who'd interviewed him earlier. The matter was resolved, and he moved on to the emails.

He wasn't surprised when he received follow-up emails and had to reply to those as well. Thankfully, no response came from the printed letter.

When Mrs. Morghentaler came back into the room thirty minutes later with his results, Alistair was wiped.

"At this time, we would like to go forward. If you do not, the car will take you back to your hotel in Aberdeen," said Mrs. Morgenthaler, repeating her earlier statement almost verbatim. She probably did this on the weekly basis.

"I'd like to go forward," replied Alistair.

"Lovely, I'll have Miss Parker show you to the rooms you'll be sharing with Mr. Murphy."

"So, Derek is going forward too?" asked Alistair. It was a foolish question, but one he thought a regular applicant might ask.

"Indeed. Your things will be sent up in a moment. Tomorrow morning, before breakfast, we'll proceed with the Drug and Alcohol Tests and the Biometric screening," she said. She handed him a large white envelope.

"You'll find a preliminary contract outlining our initial offer in the envelope. Take some time this evening to go over it and annotate it. We'll discuss any changes you might need after breakfast."

Before he could ask, she added, "You may discuss the offer with Mr. Murphy."

She walked him to the door where Miss Parker, the lady who had greeted them earlier was waiting.

"Glad to see you are still with us, Mr. Callahan. Let me show you to your rooms so you can rest and refresh yourself before dinner."

CHAPTER

SEVENTEEN

WHATEVER ALISTAIR WAS EXPECTING, this wasn't it. He had just walked into the 'rooms' he was sharing with Derek, and already his bags were inside by the door; a bellhop of some sort must have delivered them. It was a two-bedroom suite with a full bath and a tiny kitchen.

Derek came out of one of the bedrooms wearing a huge grin. He spun with his arms out in the middle of the living room.

"Do you think this is what they mean by 'Courting Candidates'?" he asked.

Alistair knew what he meant, but it hadn't ever happened to him before. One of his friends had gotten offers from three different firms when he finished Uni and each had been more extravagant than the last.

"I think so!" he replied and plopped down in one of the love seats.

Derek sat across from him. "How did your interviews go? Did they keep asking if you wanted to leave?"

"Yeah. At least three times. Do you have a physical tomorrow morning?" Alistair asked.

"Yep. I hate needles!"

"Same."

They sat in silence for a while, each lost in thought, or perhaps enjoying a power nap.

There wasn't much Alistair could discuss with Derek about the case. Although he was clearly not yet part of The Master's organization, he still couldn't be trusted with the truth. There was too much at stake.

"Do you think we're the only Warlocks here?" he finally asked.

Derek sat up. "I've been wondering the same thing all day. There's been absolutely no mention of anything magic-related. I kept thinking back to my interactions with Mr. Nielsen. We mostly used email to communicate. He never once referred to magic either, but he knows I worked at the German Biochem company. That place is run by Witches and Warlocks. Though, they might also hire humans in some departments," he said.

"What did you do for him before? You said it was freelance work," asked Alistair, trying to sound casual as he played with one of the accent cushions.

"I'm not at liberty to say specifically, but it was lab work," he replied. Derek didn't look like someone who'd been doing anything sketchy or illegal. It was a normal response in his line of work.

He got up and asked, "Do you want first dibs on the shower?"

"You go ahead. I need to text my mam, so she won't be worried," replied Alistair.

"Oh! Thanks for reminding me. I should check in too. Mam's been a bit clingy since Dad died."

"That's understandable. How are *you* doing?" Alistair wondered.

Derek shrugged and looked down at his feet.

"The last couple of days have been great. I haven't thought about it as much," he replied.

Alistair sighed. "Man, I'm sorry I brought it up."

"It's okay. My dad would be so proud. He's the one who suggested I contact Mr. Nielsen in the first place. I'm just sorry he couldn't see the outcome."

"Me too," replied Alistair. He felt like a jerk. Not only because he'd reminded Derek of his grief when he finally managed to distance himself from it, but also because of how Derek's father had died. If this was indeed The Master's lair, Derek would find out sooner or later and, though Alistair had nothing to do with it, he felt guilty by association.

Thankfully, Derek left the room and Alistair didn't need to look at his sad expression to know how his friend was feeling.

He got up, grabbed his bags, and took them into the other bedroom. It was clean and well decorated, though Alistair couldn't say what style it was. The furnishings fit with the old castle without seeming antiquated. It worked.

He took out his phone and checked in with his mom and with the MFO. It felt pathetic that the only people he had to text were his mom and his employer. He would like to be in a relationship with the right someone. But his job at the MFO often meant moving around a lot, hiding his true identity, and lying about pretty much everything. Not the best conditions for a romantic liaison.

He went back to the living room to get his contract and slipped it out of the envelope on the way back to his room. It was thick, indexed, and detailed. The tasks were still rather generic, but everything else was clearly outlined. Compensation, performance reviews, schedule, vacations, and other benefits

When he heard Derek say the bathroom was free, he placed the contract on the small desk and gathered his toiletries.

There was still enough hot water to wash away the stresses of the day. Alistair wondered if there was any way he could accept the job offer, not just as a cover. It sounded like a truly amazing opportunity. Then he laughed at himself, realizing that was precisely the point! While he was conning them into hiring him so he could infiltrate The Master's inner circle, they were likely doing the same to him.

Who in their right mind would hire a twenty-two-year-old with one year of experience for such a high-profile job?

Get real!

Things were different for Derek. He had always been a top-tier student and it was normal for him to be recruited by a top-tier company. Alistair's guilt was back with a new reason to add to the pile of why he was a jerk. The dream job Derek thought he was getting wasn't real. It was just a ploy to get him to sign on to some satanic brotherhood.

Then again, Alistair had no idea how Derek would react. Vulnerable as he was, he might leap at the chance to associate with his father's former pals. There really was no telling.

Alistair tried to relax. He was overthinking it again and taking on problems that weren't his to solve. He had to stay on task.

When he came out of the shower, he saw Derek was dressed in trousers and a dress shirt with no tie. That seemed like appropriate attire, and he did the same.

At six-thirty, someone knocked on the door. Derek opened the door and let in a lovely girl about their age, dressed in a neat wool dress. Alistair recognized her as one of the people Derek had lunch with.

"This is Kenya," he smiled.

Alistair held out a hand and said, "Nice to meet you, I'm Alistair."

"Nice to meet you too. I've come to take you to dinner. We'll be eating in the staff dining room tonight."

"Are we dressed ok?" asked Derek, pointing at his outfit.

"Yes, it's fine. Most people will still be wearing their work clothes. Some will have jeans, but no one will be wearing full suits, so it's good you changed," she explained.

"Perfect, let's go. I'm famished," said Derek, reaching for the door but Kenya put a hand up to stop him.

"Before we go, I need to explain a few things. First, you'll need to wear these lanyards around your necks." She produced them from her pocket and gave them each one. They simply said 'Visitor'. "It lets the regular staff know not to discuss sensitive information with you or in your presence. I hope you understand," she said, biting her lip.

"Yes, of course," replied Alistair.

"That being said, everyone, including the regular staff is encouraged to avoid talking about work after six p.m. The work is fascinating, but the days are long and can sometimes be grueling. The administration wants us to clock out and relax when the day is done, the way it is for those who go home at the end of the day."

"That sounds sensible," said Derek. "Anything else?"

"No, that's it."

THE STAFF DINING room wasn't nearly as fancy as the executive dining room, but it was still very posh. There had to be at least three hundred people in the room spread out over the large ballroom. Did some of the employees have dinner before they left or were these only the ones who lived at the castle? How big was this place!

The food was served cafeteria-style from two different stations at either end of the room. "Is it the same food at both ends?' asked Derek. Alistair has been wondering the same thing. Kenya said that it was, and they lined up to the one closest to them.

While in line, Alistair saw Helmut and Josette and was invited to join them at their table.

He was going to check if that was alright with Derek, but the guy was engrossed in what Kenya was saying and wasn't paying him the least bit of attention. It was safe to assume he would be fine in her pleasant company.

Dinner with Helmut, Josette, and their other friends was great. Alistair noticed no one gave their last names, and conversations stayed light and friendly.

He declined an invitation to an after-dinner board game party. Though he would have loved that, he wanted to look over his contract and go to bed early since he was pretty sure he'd have to get up early for the blood tests.

Before heading back to the room, he stopped by Derek's table.

"I'll be up soon, you go on ahead," he said, without breaking eye contact with Kenya. Here was another incentive for Derek to accept Vardo Venture's offer of employment.

When he got to the hall, Alistair retraced his steps back to their suite easily enough and let himself in. They hadn't locked the door as there hadn't been a key provided. Other than his phone and wallet, which he always kept on him, there wasn't much to steal anyway.

The rooms appeared undisturbed, but he did a quick sweep to ensure that he was alone.

He was about to check his phone messages when a slip of paper was shoved under his door. It was tomorrow's schedule. Blood and urine tests at six a.m., biometric screening at six-thirty, breakfast at seven, followed by a meeting to review the results. Next would be contract negotiations. If they came to an agreement, a final contract would be signed. A comprehensive facility tour was scheduled for after lunch. Departure was set for four p.m.

Alistair updated the MFO, confirmed their Sunday night booking at the hotel, and sent his mom a text to say he'd be home on Monday.

CHAPTER

EIGHTEEN

ALISTAIR AND DEREK left the castle on Sunday with signed contracts. They would get their affairs in order, pack some of their things, and return in a few days. They could have waited to begin the following week, but Derek was eager to begin this new chapter in his life. Alistair was eager to crack this case; it was taking longer than he'd anticipated.

This phase of Alistair's mission had been a success. He'd been hired by the company and would be living at the castle, but he had yet to be approached by anyone connected to The Master. Only time would tell.

When they returned on Wednesday afternoon, Alistair was expecting the driver to stop and provide them with a fresh eye mask. Then, he remembered that some employees drove to and from work, so they obviously knew how to get there.

The perky Miss Parker was waiting with their key cards.

"Don't lose them or lend them to a co-worker. They've been calibrated to you and your role," she said. Then, she took two brand new cell phones and handed them out.

"This is your work phone. You should leave your personal phone in your rooms. Speaking of which," she paused and retrieved a pair of keys, "these are your room keys. It's alright if I've put you together in the same room, right?"

They nodded and took the keys.

She took her own phone and highlighted the Vardo-specific features including a map of the facility, a personnel directory, an HR portal, an events calendar, and other useful apps.

"If you tap this one, you can have food sent to your room instead of eating in the cafeteria."

"Cool," said Derek. "I'm not always up for chatting."

"Same!" replied Alistair.

"There are various outings and activities on weekends. If you want a ride into town to get groceries or grab dinner, you'll see the shuttle times on this app," she pointed to a bus-shaped app. "Anyway, I'm sure you boys will figure it out."

Alistair opened the map and pretended he wanted to know how to get to their room. He thanked Miss Parker and left with Derek following on his heels.

As far as he could tell, this was indeed a map of the facility, but not of the entire castle. Vardo Ventures seemed to be taking up the western half of the castle above ground, and the entire length of it underground. It might take a little time, but Alistair was determined to do as much snooping as he could manage without getting caught. It would be challenging since the location tracker on the phone showed your position. That was useful for getting around, but not so much when you planned on going to places you weren't supposed to. He was going to have to memorize the map and ditch the phone when he explored.

They settled into their suite, unpacked, and joined their new friends for dinner. This time, Alistair wasn't going to refuse any after-dinner activity even if it was a game of charades.

It was TV night. They were showing Twilight Zone episodes in the old theater. There was even popcorn! By nine-thirty, everyone started to say goodnight.

WHEN ALISTAIR GOT to his room, he opened the schedule app. Mrs. Morgenthaler had been right. The days *were* long, but there were many opportunities to take breaks throughout the day.

On weekdays, breakfast was served at six a.m., and work started promptly at seven. They had a seventy-five-minute lunch break that they could take any time between eleven and three, and the day ended at five-thirty p.m. Dinner was served at six p.m. and was available to all employees whether they lived there or not.

Every day, they also had seventy-five minutes of self-care time, which couldn't be carried over. It could be broken up into mini breaks, tacked onto lunch, or to let them start later or finish earlier. When Alistair clicked on it, he was offered various choices such as getting a massage, going to the gym, taking a nap, or speaking with a therapist. All activities were complimentary, so long as they were booked using the app.

Alistair decided he'd take a long lunch the next day and go exploring. He pulled up the map to locate the gym and other places of interest. Tomorrow he would get the lay of the land.

CHAPTER
NINETEEN

IT TOOK Alistair a week to get his bearings, learn the routines, and find the access routes to the parts of the castle that weren't on the map. His best strategy was to leave his phone in a bathroom, hidden with an invisibility charm, and use his time gift to explore without being gone too long.

Meanwhile, he enjoyed the work and had been flagged for exemplary performance twice.

He and Derek were still no closer to figuring out whether they were the only Warlocks at Vardo. If there were magical humans in the administration, they would easily identify the magical hires from their blood tests. There were markers in the blood, though only advanced tests could identify which magical bloodline they were from. Based on the size of the lab in the basement, it was safe to say this facility could handle such an undertaking.

Derek loved his job and never wanted to leave. They had him hook, line, and sinker. It was everything: the job, the perks, and Kenya.

There had been a few clauses about workplace relationships in the contract. They weren't prohibited, but there was a reporting process.

And as it turned out, there *were* other magical humans around. It was Kenya who invited Derek, who in turn invited Alistair, to a get-together for Witches and Warlocks. As Derek and Kenya got closer, they disclosed that part of their background to each other.

Kenya described how she and like-minded friends got together once or twice per week in a secure location. Alistair wondered if this was his way in. Was it an activity set up by Vardo to cater to their magical employees? Or was this The Master's way of recruiting minions. Either way, now they knew they weren't the only Warlocks.

Alistair was surprised that Derek agreed to it; it seemed sketchy, even to him.

Ah, the power of love.

Lo and behold, the meeting took place in a room behind the theater. On the map, Alistair could see that the back of the theater ran along the line where the castle was split in half. The door they entered led out of Vardo Ventures and, Alistair hoped, into The Master's lair.

His patience was rewarded. Upon entering, they were provided with plain black robes. It seemed like a formal, organized affair. Once they'd put them on, they were asked to make a blood oath to never reveal what they saw or heard at one of the meetings.

Alistair and Derek looked at each other, unsure.

"It's no worse than the non-disclosure agreement you signed. This is just a bit more dramatic," said Kenya, holding a ritual athame.

"And a little less sanitary," replied Derek.

Kenya raised an eyebrow and pursed her lips. She held out the blade in front of her, but away from the guys and snapped her fingers. A flame rose up from her finger and she passed it over the blade three times and blew on the flame to extinguish it like it was a smoking gun. She turned the blade and presented the hilt to Derek.

When he didn't immediately take it, she put a hand on her hip and turned to Alistair. Alistair took the knife, made a small cut in the fleshy part of his hand, and said, "I solemnly swear to remain quiet about what I see and hear tonight."

He gave her the knife and closed his fist over the bowl on the table and let a few drops spill, then grabbed one of the paper napkins and pressed it to the wound.

Kenya nodded, satisfied, wiped the blade, and repeated her sanitation ritual for Derek's benefit.

A blood oath was difficult to fake. It was all in the wording. The way he'd worded his oath, he wouldn't be able to *say* anything about the meetings, but he *could* text about it.

Once Derek was sworn in, they entered the main room where a dozen or so robed and hooded figures sat quietly in a circle. Kenya pointed to three seats and put a finger to her lips for them to remain quiet. She then pointed to her eyes and directed their gaze to an empty seat across from them. Derek and Alistair nodded and waited for whoever was supposed to arrive.

The room was bare, aside from the chairs, which were gathered under a large chandelier to provide enough light to find their way, but not enough to see anyone's face clearly. A door opened from the other end of the room and another hooded figure entered.

They made their way to the empty seat but did not immediately sit down. Extending their hands to either side, they made an upward sweeping motion. In unison, all in attendance rose.

"I am Brother Jameson, a loyal member of The Master's Inner Circle. Have you come to join him?" said a rather young-sounding voice.

In unison, the assembly replied, "Yes."

He put his arms out again, made a downward motion, and everyone sat.

Alistair wondered if this was the missing boy from Harding Academy, the one that had disappeared after his altercations with Tom in the dungeon and the West Tower. One look at his face would confirm this, but Jameson's face stayed in the shadows.

"Who among you are here for the first time?" Brother Jameson asked.

A few raised their hands, including Derek and Alistair.

"Welcome, new friends. You have been invited to this meeting to hear about another recruitment opportunity. If, after you have heard what I have to say, you do not wish to go forward, simply exit the way you came, leave the robe, and do not speak of this to anyone. Your blood oath should ensure you comply with the latter."

They nodded and put their hands down.

"Let's begin. The Master is a Blood Mage. He can heal the sick and wounded, control others through their blood, and even raise the dead."

He paused for effect. There were a few gasps and Alistair heard someone say a quick 'yeah' under their breath.

"He is recruiting followers to help him rebuild the magical community to its former glory. For too long, we've been hiding in the shadows, letting humans lead the world."

The assembly made signs of agreement.

"What have they done with their power? They've destroyed our natural resources and made themselves sick. They've polluted their bodies the way they've polluted our rivers, lakes, and oceans."

He was gaining momentum; people were cheering now.

"The Master proposes a new world order, one where Witches and Warlocks would rule; where all magical and non-magical species are equal, and where food, shelter, and healing are free to all who request it."

The assembly started to clap. Alistair was moved by Jameson's speech as much as anyone in the room. The guy was good. He put up a hand to silence them.

"The Master needs leaders, ambassadors, healers, scientists, lawyers, and all manner of quality players like yourselves for his team. Who here wants to join the winning team?"

Everyone rose, including Alistair. As far as he could determine, Jameson wasn't charming them in any magical sense. He was using good old-fashioned psychological propaganda. How many of these powerful Witches and Warlocks felt truly powerless to change the world? They would follow the piper to their deaths thinking they were here to make the world a better place.

It was one of the reasons that Alistair had joined the MFO. He wanted to help, but the never-ending secrecy hindered the scope of their good works, often being limited to the magical community only.

"I'm happy to see we've found progressive thinkers to join our ranks. Come, follow me. The Master is waiting," he said as he rose and headed toward the door he had arrived from.

There was a hush of excitement as everyone filed in behind him. As Alistair got in line, he noticed that some people rolled up their sleeves and showed their upper arms to the figure waiting at the door. He nodded to them and went out into the hall.

Alistair, Derek, and the other new recruits were given black sacs to place over their heads. It was too late to back out now. Alistair complied and let himself be led away by a strange hand.

CHAPTER

TWENTY

TOM SWALLOWED AUDIBLY. He was face-to-face with The Master and had a clear view of his features. It had to be his grandfather, Brendan. Though he looked much older than sixty. This man looked like he was well over ninety.

Tom didn't know how to respond to the telling of his tale. The anguish in The Master's voice seemed genuine. When he placed a steadying hand on Tom's shoulder, it took everything he had in him not to recoil.

"Would you like to sit down, Sir?" Tom asked, hoping to extricate himself from the man's touch.

The Master looked into Tom's eyes, as though searching his soul.

"You're a lot like him," The Master said. "Your father was kind and generous, but ultimately weak. And it had nothing to do with his illness."

The Master let go of Tom and stepped away from him. He grimaced, either in pain or distaste, as he pulled himself to his full height and started pacing around his captive audience. When he resumed his tale, Tom sat back down.

"I already know you're stronger, Tom. You've proved it on more than one occasion."

He paused and slipped a hand into the folds of his robe and took out a small object.

My ring!

"You see, Tom. After the unfortunate incident with your father, I needed to test you in a way that wouldn't put your life in jeopardy. Young as you are, you haven't had a chance to produce heirs yet. So, you are my last hope."

He resumed pacing, changing directions this time. He didn't look at Mandy, Zaina, Benny, or Arturo when he spoke, but Tom wondered if he was making sure they were still securely fastened to their chairs. He wouldn't put it past any of them to be trying to get out of their ropes and away from this melodrama.

The Master held the ring between his thumb and forefinger.

"It was very clever of me to charm the ring," he started.

Tom's head whipped up. "But the ring was examined by Head-master Lianon and Professor Montague. They both declared that it was just a ring."

"*Just a ring*? I'll have you know that it was Petunia's ring. The one I gave to her when Conor was born. Can't you see how the vines form a 'C'?" he said, moving closer and placing the ring in front of Tom's face.

"Dad said it was a 'C' for Callahan," Tom replied.

The Master huffed and spat out, "An unfortunate coincidence. To think that my entire legacy bore another man's name. It's enough to make me vomit."

Tom frowned. What was the crazy man saying now?

"I don't understand, Sir. Did you go back in time?" he asked.

"I'm getting ahead of myself. The ring was infused with my blood, hence Blood Magick. It's a magic older than that Montague Witch, though not older than the High Elf. I'm surprised he didn't pick up on it. Then again, he was in his bubble school when he examined it and probably didn't have access to his full abilities. "

Tom shot a look to Zaina. She was listening attentively and nodding at Tom; it made him think she was telling him to keep the old man talking.

"So, that's how I've had Blood Magick this whole time?" Tom started to worry.

"Indeed. Have you been able to use it since your ring was taken?" he asked.

Tom had to think about it. He'd been busy with school, classes, and new friends.

"I haven't had a chance," he replied, still deep in thought. "Why did you switch the rings then? I'm sure I could do Blood Magick even after you switched the rings," Tom said, trying to recall.

"The second ring had more power in it. I wanted to see how you handled it. As I said, I've been taking extra precautions with you," replied The Master.

"It made me mean, paranoid, and depressed. I'm not sure I handled it very well," huffed Tom.

The Master chuckled and turned to Tom from his spot behind Benny. His friend's eyes grew large as he tried to crane his neck to see how close The Master was. For the most part, The Master was still ignoring the others; it was almost like he had another pair of eyes keeping tabs on everyone at once, in secret.

"That wasn't the ring. That was likely a post-traumatic stress response."

"I felt a lot better after Emmet took it from me," replied Tom.

"You felt better because you had something, *someone* to blame for everything that was happening. You felt better because you had someone to talk to, someone you felt you could trust," explained The Master.

Tom had to admit that it was a logical possibility. He'd been played on so many levels, it was embarrassing. That's when a most distressing thought occurred to him. *If I have no power, other than Traveling magic, without the ring? How am I supposed to defeat The Master?*

CHAPTER
TWENTY-ONE

"HOLD OUT YOUR LEFT ARM," said Jameson.

Alistair had been led to another room. It was warm. But the heat radiating around his darkened blindfold had not been comforting. He could smell the wood burning and hear the crackle of the fire to his right.

He extended his arm in front of him.

"State your full name," the boy said.

"Alistair Callahan."

"Are you Imogene and Liam Callahan's son?" another voice asked. It was older and dry as sandpaper. It had to be The Master.

"Yes, I am, Sir," he answered.

"How interesting."

"Are you ready to join The Master on his mission to save the world from itself?" asked Jameson, grasping his arm roughly and pulling up the sleeve of the robe.

Alistair jerked his arm back unconsciously, but Jameson held fast.

There was only one good answer at this point.

"I am."

He braced himself for what came next. Would they cut him? Give him a tattoo?

He found out soon enough when he felt the searing hot metal press against his flesh. He struggled, but Jameson had him in an iron grip. He bit the inside of his cheek to keep from crying out. The smell of burning flesh made him nauseous and he swayed a little.

"You're one of us, now," Jameson said as he yanked the black pillowcase off his head.

Alistair blinked as his eyes adjusted to the change in lighting.

"Open your mouth, Brother Alistair, and receive The Master," said Jameson solemnly.

Alistair turned to look at the boy in confusion. There was no scenario where that wasn't both creepy and frightening.

Jameson, who had retreated a few steps away, rushed him and forcefully opened his mouth.

The Master came closer and peered at him. His head was tilted back, and he couldn't get a close look at the man before him. "You look like your grandfather, Brian," he said before poking his finger with a dagger and dropping a single drop of blood into Alistair's mouth. He smiled and moved away as Jameson pressed on his jaw to make him close his mouth. "Swallow," he commanded.

Bile had risen from his gut and made his mouth water, so the command was easy enough to obey. Once he had complied, Jameson pushed his shoulders down, "Now, bow to your Master."

Alistair fell to his knees and bowed, trying not to retch. "Master," he said.

"Rise, Brother Alistair. We are equals in the New Order," claimed The Master.

When Alistair rose, The Master was casting an inquisitive look at Jameson.

"I apologize for Jameson's lack of finesse. He's not usually so ill-tempered. I think he may be jealous," said The Master.

"Why would I be jealous?" countered Jameson.

"Because I've found another candidate," replied The Master.

"Candidate for what?" asked Alistair warily.

"To be my successor, of course."

CHAPTER
TWENTY-TWO

NO WONDER The Master was so relaxed. With his friends tied up and scared they'd get hurt and Tom nearly powerless, there really wasn't anything to worry about.

"So, I guess I passed your tests. Now what? Why am I here? You still haven't told me what you want from me," said Tom.

"Yes, you passed all my tests. You are my true heir and the next Blood Mage."

"I've already inherited your Estate when Dad died. I was told that you had died as well. So, the real question is, when and how did you plan on transferring your 'gift'? What happens if I don't want it? Is this 'gift' the reason you look so old and frail?" quipped Tom.

The Master flinched; Tom had struck a nerve.

"*Having* the gift makes you the most powerful Sorcerer in the world. It ensures perfect health and longevity, lets you heal the sick and the wounded, control your enemies, and raise the dead."

"I've heard the sales pitch before. It sounds too good to be true. There must be a catch," replied Tom.

"There's no catch, but there's a cost. Using the gift depletes you and, until you can build up your reserves again, you are vulnerable to attack. That is why I have created the Brotherhood, to protect me when I cannot protect myself."

"How can you be sure they won't kill you themselves? How have they not already bled you while you slept?" asked Tom.

He pinched the bridge of his nose in frustration. It was like assembling a puzzle where you didn't have all the pieces laid out.

"When they are sworn in, they are given a drop of my blood. That single drop enables me to control them, or rather, the blood that courses through them. They are also branded. The blood is enough to heal a wound, but not the mark. It increases their faith in my ability to heal them, or their loved ones, should they ever require it."

Tom wanted to hurl. Next, the old coot would be telling him that he was secretly a vampire and now so were his disciples.

"But doesn't that deplete you as well? Is that why you've aged so much" asked Tom. Desperately trying to understand it all.

"Blood renews faster than depleted powers. It's like any transfusion, you just need to rest and drink water. No, I appear older than I am because I wasn't meant to stay in this body for so long."

Wait, what?

"I'm not sure I know what you mean," said Tom, trying to remain calm.

"Normally, the gift is passed on after the prospective heir has produced an heir of their own. So far, it's always been passed down to the males. It would be entirely too messy for females to receive this gift. Women have their own blessed gifts.

Once you were born, I broached the topic with your father. He outright refused. I decided to give him some time to ponder the prospect, faked my own death, and set about finding another suitable candidate in case I couldn't sway his mind. I thought perhaps we might not need to be related for the transfer to work.

I left Ireland and used some hidden assets to start a company called Vardo Ventures, based out of Norway."

He smiled to himself, as though this was a private joke.

"The purpose of the company was to have access to people's blood so I might find someone who had the right genetic markers."

"And did you find anyone?" asked Tom.

"I spent a decade analyzing blood. When a candidate had over a ninety percent match, I'd have my team extend an invitation."

Tom shuddered at the thought of that invitation.

"None of them were viable subjects," he concluded.

"You mean they died, you killed them," Tom choked out the words.

"They signed the paperwork; they understood the risks. Their families were well compensated," replied The Master as though this had been a simple clinical trial gone wrong.

"How many innocent people did you murder in the name of science?" asked Tom, utterly revolted. He heard a whimper and turned to see who it was. It was Mandy. She'd been stoic until now, but this last bit had apparently done her in.

Zaina, however, looked mad enough to spit nails. Benny had either fallen asleep or passed out and Arturo's eyes were closed. Perhaps he was astral projecting somewhere, or meditating, or silently calling reinforcements. Tom hoped he wasn't merely praying for help to arrive.

"If I had been able to pass on the gift to your father, those deaths could have been avoided!" exclaimed The Master, clearly affronted at being accused of needlessly murdering innocent people.

"Now it's my father's fault that those people died? Next, you'll be blaming me!" shouted Tom.

"When I heard he was sick, I came back. I begged him to take the gift, if not for himself, then for his family. If he could be healed, he could see you and your sister grow up."

"He didn't need to take the gift to be healed, though. Why didn't you just heal him?" asked Tom, tears streaming down his cheeks now at the thought that he might have had more time with his dad.

"I *did* heal him!" yelled The Master, his own frustration evident.

"Then, why is he dead?" screamed Tom.

"Because he killed *me*."

CHAPTER

TWENTY-THREE

JAMESON PUSHED him out the door where another initiate waited his turn. As Alistair walked down the hall, he saw Kenya standing by a door. When he reached her, she motioned for him to go in. It was the room behind the theater.

Another hooded figure beckoned him from the other end of the room where he and Derek had arrived.

"Brother Alistair, place the robe in the basket. Another will be provided when you return," he said gesturing at the large laundry basket in the corner.

"Report to work as usual tomorrow. After dinner, return here for further instructions."

He opened the door that led back into the theater and Alistair walked out.

He went back to their suite. Finding it empty, he went to his room to update the MFO. This was a huge breakthrough. The Master's cryptic words about succession would, at the very least, ensure that he rose quickly through the ranks until he was part of the inner circle.

Once his duty had been dispatched, he brushed his teeth and gargled with mouthwash. He jumped in the shower and tried to wash the creepiness of the night away. He had planned on disinfecting the wound on his palm and the brand, but the wound had healed and the skin over the brand was smooth and healthy. It looked like a tattoo, only a shade darker than his skin. He hadn't bothered to look at what it was they had branded him with. The circular symbol was stamped a few inches above the elbow where it would be covered by a t-shirt. It was an inverted pentagram with a drop of blood dripping from the bottom tip.

Alistair put on his pajamas and got into bed. He left his door open and grabbed a book to read while he waited for Derek. He couldn't focus on his book. He kept going through the evening's events in his mind. He wished he had the gift of illusion or a spycam so he could go back to observe things he might have missed. Like The Master's face.

When Derek still hadn't returned at ten o'clock, Alistair got up, locked the front door, and went to bed. It seemed that Derek had gotten lucky.

ALISTAIR ATTENDED the nightly meetings for the rest of the week. One meeting explained how they would be contributing to the Brotherhood, and another provided a timeline of concerted actions that would begin as soon as The Master found his successor.

It had thrown Alistair when the Master had mentioned he might be a candidate for succession. Obviously, Tom Callahan was the next Blood Mage and his successor. So, why would The Master have suggested it?

Perhaps The Master was rethinking his options after his first encounter with Tom. Or perhaps he meant a successor for Vardo Ventures. At any rate, Alistair was pretty sure that Tom wanted no part of leading The Master's army into world domination.

Meanwhile, Alistair saw less and less of Derek. He and Kenya were spending almost all their time together. Derek would drop by the room for a change of clothes or sometimes they would meet up for a quick chat to touch base. Alistair was happy that Derek seemed to have found his place at Vardo, and with Kenya, and he hoped it wouldn't end badly for them.

The Master's propaganda was alluring. Each Brother and Sister was promised compensation, both monetary and in the form of positions of power within the new order. This was in addition to their already sizeable salaries and benefits.

Due to the flexible nature of their schedules, the additional tasks required of The Master's Vardo followers were easily integrated into their daily schedules.

One Saturday afternoon, Alistair was invited to have tea with The Master to discuss his contribution to the cause.

Alistair had expected it to be another group affair. But he found himself alone with The Master when the tea tray was served. Though Alistair was sure that there were a number of sunny parlors and sitting rooms elsewhere in the castle, The Master received him in what appeared to be his study. He was seated behind his desk, a fair distance from Alistair, his face hidden in shadows again.

"Shall I pour, Sir?" Alistair asked, to break the silence.

The Master stared at him for a moment before replying, "Please, help yourself. I'm neither hungry nor thirsty."

Neither was Alistair. But it would have seemed rude to decline at this point. He poured himself a cup and grabbed a scone for good measure. The Master was still observing him intently. Alistair bit into the scone and took a sip of the tea, hoping neither were poisoned nor laced with a truth serum.

He had gotten lucky, perhaps too lucky, so far.

"When last we spoke, you said I looked like my grandfather. Did you know him well?" he asked finally.

The Master nodded. "Yes. I was sorry to hear that he passed. We were close at one time, as close as brothers you might say," he replied, chuckling to himself.

Alistair continued to drink his tea and munch on the scone, waiting for The Master to tell him why he was summoned to meet here.

"You are doing well at Vardo Ventures," he said finally, watching him eat. "Do you enjoy your work?"

"Yes, Sir. It's very stimulating and rewarding. I have excellent colleagues. Thank you for the opportunity," replied Alistair in complete sincerity.

"Good, good. As you know, each of my followers will have a role to play in the new world we are building for our magical brethren. Have you given a thought as to what part you would like to play?"

The question took him off guard. He had expected The Master to assign him a task as he had to all the Brothers and Sisters. As far as Alistair knew, no one had been given a choice. Why him? Why now?

"I'm certain that you would know better than me how I could best serve the cause, Sir," he replied, trying to swallow his scone.

"Nonetheless, if given the choice, where do you see yourself?"

Alistair put his teacup on the tray and made a show of thinking about it before replying, "I would like to be at your side, Sir."

The Master smiled and sat back in his chair. He turned in his winged-back chair and sat facing the fireplace across the room. The heat seemed to gravitate to The Master, like life to a black hole.

"I would like you to oversee the Intelligence team. I have recruited several able agents, but I require an analyst. I believe you would be well-suited to the position of espionage. What do you think?"

Did he know? Was he baiting him? Or was this the natural conclusion to the extensive testing Alistair had undergone for his job at Vardo.

Alistair arranged his features into what he hoped was a surprised, yet honored look.

"It would be an honor, Sir. I've always wanted to work for the secret service," he replied truthfully.

"Well then, it's settled. I'll have Brother Jameson show you to your new office. It's in the library. Your agents will report to you every day at noon. You will receive their intelligence and then assign tasks as you see fit. Beyond that daily meeting, you are free to manage your own schedule.

It's best you continue to report to work as usual, but you may have your meals delivered to your office if you wish. And, if you prefer, you can work in the evening. It's entirely up to you."

"Don't I need to attend the nightly meetings?"

"No."

"Thank you, Sir. I won't let you down," he replied, all too ready to leave.

A knock at the door signaled Jameson's arrival. Alistair took this as his cue to leave. He rose, bowed to The Master, and left.

HIS OFFICE WAS MORE than adequate. In fact, it was better than the one he initially had at Vardo. Though much smaller, it resembled The Master's study, complete with a stone fireplace and two winged-back chairs in front of it.

Jameson didn't linger after opening the door and handing him a set of keys. "If there's anything you need, just ask one of the Brothers."

Alistair thanked him and closed the door.

Several reports were stacked on his desk. Before tackling them, Alistair swept the room for devices. When he found none, he spelled the room to make it soundproof, then applied a charm to the door and windows to ensure that, should anyone manage to come in or look in through a window, all they would see is Alistair reading at his desk. It was a clever illusion spell provided by the MFO for use on undercover missions.

He took out his personal phone and updated the MFO on his new status.

CHAPTER
TWENTY-FOUR

"WE NEED to get back to school," replied Professor Hilltop upon hearing what Professor Montague had to say.

"I agree. It's one thing to take down wards and distract a few guards, but we're too old to launch an attack on these young Warlocks, let alone The Master. Besides, there's no telling how he would retaliate should we even try," said Professor Bellamy, wringing her hands.

"I take issue at being called too old. We more than took care of those pups earlier, but I must agree with a plan to retreat. We are sorely outnumbered," retorted Professor Hilltop.

"That's settled. Does everyone have their Portal token?" asked Professor Montague.

Professors Hilltop and Bellamy produced theirs as their colleague held hers up.

"Let's meet at Miss Clementine's office," she said, before throwing her token a few feet in front of her. The flash of light was blinding in the dark forest beyond the castle and the teachers shielded their eyes. Professor Montague waited as the swirl grew bigger, crossing the threshold when the Portal had reached its maximum height. As soon as she was through, the Portal spun in on itself and closed.

Professor Hilltop motioned for Professor Bellamy to go next. He cast one last look around the woods and toward the castle and tossed in his coin.

❧

"I DON'T THINK I should open a Portal directly into the ballroom," said Lady Mathilda.

"No, it's not safe for you or the children," agreed Miss Clementine.

"Our Portals weren't meant for covert operations. Even if I managed to enter unseen, I could only take one of them with me before the Portal closed again. The Master could very well move the others before I could return for the next student. I could enlist my sister and Headmaster Lianon, I'm sure they would help, but that is still only three of us," said the High Elf.

"I could astral project and go back to the castle if one of the children manages to astral project. Of the four, Mandy is the most skilled, I believe. She would know how to come here for help, but someone would need to be here, in astral form, to receive her," said Professor Montague.

"I think we may need you here, but perhaps we can enlist some of the other teachers to take turns and keep us updated about what's going on in the ballroom. If we rotate every hour, the outgoing teacher can give us an update. Unless there's an emergency, then they should alert us immediately," suggested Miss Clementine.

The others nodded. "Professor Bellamy, could you take care of setting that up?"

The older Witch leaped to her feet and replied, "Of course. I'll see to it straight away," she announced on her way to the door.

It was getting late. Miss Clementine ordered tea from the kitchen and then called the CEMB to update them on the latest developments. She requested permission to send Lady Mathilda to Alistair's office so he might offer further assistance to the children. She hung up and sat at her desk to wait for their go-ahead.

"As soon as they've confirmed it, you can Portal into Alistair's office," she said to Lady Mathilda.

CHAPTER
TWENTY-FIVE

ARTURO CLOSED his eyes and went into a trance. If there was ever a time to master astral projection, this was it. He heard The Master's monologue fade in the background as he breathed in and out the way he'd been taught.

After what seemed like an eternity and a plethora of false starts, he finally managed it.

He was out of his body, staring back at it. He was trying to remember how to project himself back to school in the hopes of meeting Professor Montague or another teacher in astral form when he heard someone whisper his name.

He cocked his head and wondered if one of his friends was addressing him in the real world. He looked around at his friends. Zaina was glaring at The Master, furiously working on the ropes binding her hands. Mandy seemed to be chanting silently, her lips barely moving. Perhaps she too was trying to loosen the ropes.

He turned to Benny and was surprised to see another astral projection in the room. Benny was waving at him from above his body. Motioning for him to follow.

Arturo was impressed. If he thought he'd meet any of their group on the astral plane, he'd have voted for anyone but Benny. Perhaps he'd been too harsh in discounting the sensitive boy.

He followed Benny out of the room and into the empty hall.

"Finally! I've been out wandering for so long I thought I might not be able to get back into my body," he whispered.

"You don't need to whisper, Benny. No one can see or hear us unless they are on the astral plane."

"Right. Anyway. I've had a fly around and the teachers are gone. However, there aren't that many minions lying about. There are no more than ten on this floor and, as you can see, no one is guarding the doors," said Benny, pointing to the doors they'd been pushed through earlier.

"That's good a reckon, Benny," replied Arturo.

Benny beamed at the praise.

"Do you know how to get to Harding from here?" he asked.

"Short of flying there? No, I don't," said Arturo.

"I don't either. And I don't even know the way from here," replied Benny, dejectedly.

"I guess we'll need to work out a plan ourselves, then."

They were silent for a moment, each thinking of ways to extricate themselves from this mess.

"Who died?" said Mandy, seeing their long faces as she floated into the hallway.

Benny yelped in surprise. "Mandy!"

"Hey Benny, I thought you had passed out," she said.

"Nah, I'm just a good actor!" he exclaimed.

"Were the tears part of the act?" quipped Arturo.

Mandy shot him a look as Benny hung his head in embarrassment. "No. Those were real. I was really frightened."

Mandy glared at Arturo and tried to comfort Benny as best she could, "We're going to get out of this, Benny. I promise."

"How?" he asked.

"I have a plan!"

"Great, because we've got nothing," replied Benny.

"I was formulating a plan when you arrived," said Arturo, clearly miffed to be lumped in with Benny.

"Let's hear it," said Mandy.

"If we can get out of our bindings, we can distract The Master enough to get out of there," he started before Mandy cut him off.

"You guys missed a lot while you were flying out here. We can't leave Tom to deal with the psycho, he's powerless without the ring."

"Huh? What do you mean?"

"It's a long story and I need to get back, so I won't miss more of the important stuff. But basically, the only Blood Magick Tom had was in the ring. The Master is preparing to transfer it to Tom, but I get the feeling that killing him isn't a good idea. What we need to do is get the ring back to Tom somehow, so he has a fighting chance, and somehow keep The Master from doing the transfer. So far, it looks like Tom is stalling until he has all the facts."

"Okay, but how do you propose we go about it?" asked Arturo.

"I'm almost out of my bindings. The first one of us that's free needs to release the others without The Master noticing. If I can get Zaina's attention, she can call the ring to her. It's a magical artifact, it should work. If things get dicey, Benny could freeze him. It wouldn't last long, but it would help us get the ring to Tom, or quickly coordinate with him and Zaina."

"The plan isn't without merit, but what would you have me do?" asked Arturo.

Mandy gave him a funny look, like what she was about to say should have been obvious.

"You and Zaina are the strongest fighters. You both can use offensive magic way better than the rest of us. You'll wage war on The Master, of course."

Arturo nodded quickly. He couldn't hide the slight upturn of his mouth or the glee that came across his face as he rubbed his hands together in anticipation of the battle ahead.

"I'll go back, first. It's best if we don't suddenly wake up at the same time," explained Mandy before floating through the wall.

"I'll go next as I've been out the longest," said Benny. He gave Arturo a two-finger salute, which Arturo returned despite himself.

Arturo decided on another perimeter run. It was much too quiet in the castle; then again, it was past nine and The Master had dismissed the guards near the ballroom. It was just like Benny had said. If they could make it out of the room, Arturo was confident they could leave the castle unhindered.

When he got back to the hall, he saw Harding's potion master lurking about. As he approached him, Arturo was elated to see the Warlock was in astral form.

"Professor Filigree! What are you doing here?"

"Arturo! It's good to see you. Miss Clementine sent me. A few of us will take turns keeping watch so we can send help or keep the CEMB updated on the situation. What can you tell me?"

Arturo told him what had been going on and added the bits Mandy had shared before going back. The Professor nodded and replied, "Since I've been here, I heard the Master say that Tom's father had killed him. The 'gift' entered John's body but did not stick. John died and the 'gift' went back into The Master's body, reviving him. I gathered The Master was Brendan Callahan. However, Tom just called him Brön and now I'm confused."

Arturo's jaw dropped. He had missed a lot while he was trying to get out of his body and since he'd left the room.

"Okay, that makes a little sense. From what Tom said, Brön was the Witch Hunter, cursed to roam the earth as a zombie until he could find a Witch to fall in love with who would also love him back. That Witch was Petunia Callahan, Sir Anthony Callahan's wife. They met by chance, or perhaps not by chance as Brön was hunting the Witches who had escaped sanction in Vardo. Anyway, they fell in love and had three kids, one of which was Conor Callahan, Tom's ancestor. All while she was still married to Sir Anthony, who only came home once or twice per year from his many sea voyages. If what you are saying is right, then Brön is not only the origin of Blood Magick, but may also still be involved, though I'm not sure how exactly. I was told he died a few days after Conor was born."

Professor Filigree nodded.

"I see. Had he lived, he would be almost four hundred years old, which even for a Witch of that era, is old. These days, Witches rarely live past one hundred and fifty. Is there more you can tell me? I think I need to report this immediately to Miss Clementine," said the teacher.

Arturo was still trying to wrap his mind around The Master being Brön. He now wished he'd stayed to find out what that was about.

"I can't think of anything else except that Tom has no Blood Magick without his father's ring. The Master infused it to see if Tom could handle the Magick since his father could not. It seems he's been experimenting on magical humans in his underground lab here at the castle in the hopes of finding a match. So far, Tom's his only chance."

Professor Filigree told Arturo to go back into his body and sit tight, help was on the way.

CHAPTER
TWENTY-SIX

ALISTAIR HADN'T BEEN BACK in his office for thirty minutes when he got a text from the MFO asking if it was safe for Lady Mathilda to come back.

It was. He was alone and no one had noticed his absence before, but it was still unnerving. Where would the High Elf take him next?

He texted his reply and waited anxiously. While he was overjoyed at his success on the current mission, there were times when he wondered if he was truly cut out for this level of undercover work.

He'd traveled from Italy to London in the last month, then to Ireland. From there, he'd interviewed and gotten a job at an undisclosed location in Scotland, in an evil Sorcerer's castle no less.

He'd let himself be recruited by the Brotherhood, a secret elitist group serving The Master, a powerful Blood Mage, intent on world domination. To that end, he'd been indoctrinated, branded, and fed blood to ensure his compliance.

He was now heading up a team of intelligence agents who had infiltrated every tier of government in the UK, with plans to extend across Europe, then Asia, and the Americas. To say the least, it was a bit overwhelming.

He felt the air crackle around him and lowered his wards to let

Lady Mathilda Portal in and immediately drew them up again once she had arrived.

"The Brothers have captured Mandy, Zaina, Benny, and Arturo. They're tied to chairs in the ballroom with Tom and The Master," she said without preamble.

"Is Tom tied up as well?" he asked.

"Not as far as I know," she replied.

"Why haven't they tried to escape or fight back? It's five against one. Surely, they can slip out of the old man's grasp," he said. Even as he said it, he knew that The Master may be old and frail, but he could probably hold a gaggle of teenagers indefinitely.

"The Master has threatened them. If the others try anything, he'll hurt Tom. If Tom attacks him, he'll kill his friends."

"I see. How can I help?" he asked.

She filled him in on the latest developments and asked him to hurry. Alistair lowered the wards so she could leave. Once she had, he sat staring at the information on his desk, wondering which might warrant disturbing The Master.

None of it would be deemed critical.

He closed his eyes and tried to think about what might incite panic in The Master. What was his biggest secret, what did they guard most vehemently?

That's it! His location!

Alistair opened his laptop and pulled up the satellite images over the castle. He took a screenshot and fabricated a message from a scrambled email address to a partial scrambled address at the CEMB. The message read: We've found him.

Alistair printed the fake email and sped to the ballroom, hoping The Master wouldn't shoot the messenger.

CHAPTER
TWENTY-SEVEN

"THAT MAKES NO SENSE!" Tom yelled. "If *he* killed *you*, then why is he dead and you are alive!?"

Tom stood opposite The Master, near Mandy, while the older man stood near Benny.

"We were in my study, by then it was your father's study. I can only assume he thought that killing me would put an end to the curse once and for all." The Master chuckled humorlessly. "That's how he saw Blood Magick. Not as a gift, but as a curse. If he knew all I had been through to break the actual curse!"

"So what happened," said Tom through gritted teeth.

"I had just healed him. He was feeling stronger, the color was returning to his cheeks. I asked if he was reconsidering, and he remained adamant about not doing the transfer. When I said I would wait and try again with you, he grabbed the letter opener and stabbed me. He stabbed me nine times like I was a cat he wanted to make sure didn't come back!

I was too stunned to be angry or even try to stop him. I would never have thought him capable of such a thing. In the moments just before I died, I was so very proud of him even as I lamented that the gift would be lost forever.

What neither of us knew at the time, was that if you kill the host, the gift will move into the closest available host, and continue to do so until a viable match can be found.

The gift left this body and entered your father's. Though he felt and looked better, he must have not been completely healed yet. The gift couldn't take hold and exited his body. Finding no other hosts, it came back into its original body and revived it. *Me*." The Master grinned an otherworldly grin.

Tom shook his head in despair. The was no killing this monster! With every mention of the word *host*, he grew more and more certain that the madman telling his tale was not Brendan, his grandfather, but Brön the Witch Hunter. Petunia's lover. It was an allusive thought circulating his mind all throughout this mad story that suddenly hit him like the rock he threw through the garden shed.

"How old are you?" Tom asked, changing his tactic.

The Master looked at him and smiled. "I'm about sixty."

"No, that's Brendan. You're Brön, right?"

The Master clapped his hands three times. "Bravo!"

"That would make you, over three hundred years old," said Tom.

"'That sounds about right," The Master said with a chuckle.

"So, I get that I can't kill you. Otherwise, the gift may land in one of my friends and kill them. And if it lands on me, I'll turn into, well, you. Neither of those options is appealing."

"Why do you resist? Imagine all the good you could do in the world with that kind of power," exclaimed The Master, slowly inching his way toward Tom through the circle of chairs.

"But would I even be me? Or would you take over my body like you did everyone else?"

"It isn't like that. It's a much more symbiotic relationship. You may find this hard to believe, but I care for you. I care for you all as I did for my own children."

Tom didn't believe that for a second. If it were such a good deal, his father would have agreed and done it himself. If he thought he could control the power better than his own father, he would have done it.

No. John Callahan had chosen death over continuing this unholy legacy.

"Don't you need to wait until I've had a son of my own?" asked Tom, hoping he might delay the inevitable.

Before The Master could answer, there was a knock at the door. Everyone turned to look in that direction. Tom was surprised to see both Arturo and Benny's heads turn as he hadn't noticed they had awoken from their apparent slumber.

Mandy took advantage of the diversion to catch Zaina's attention. She mouthed the word 'ring' and nodded to The Master, then to Tom.

Zaina squinted, confused. To her, it looked like Mandy was smiling or showing her teeth. Tom caught on and pointed at his finger behind his back. Eventually, Zaina nodded, though she still looked confused, and wiggled her shoulders and arms to remind Mandy that they were all tied up. Mandy winked.

The knocker entered and spoke loudly. "Master, I have critical information you need to know about," said the hooded figure.

The Master extended his hand in the Brother's direction, "Come," he summoned. The minion lifted an inch off the floor and hovered over the ground as though being pulled by an invisible thread. When he came within a foot of the Master, the older man put his hand up in a stop gesture and the Brother halted with a jerk and was once again allowed to stand on his own two feet.

The look on his face was both shocked and more than a little pained. The Master turned away from him to address Tom.

"See what one drop of my blood, *our* blood, can do? Imagine if we diluted some in the water supply, the humans would be so easy to control!"

The Brother's head was bowed, but he was holding out a piece of paper. He cleared his throat and said, "Sir, it's quite urgent."

The Master sighed and turned back to the hooded figure. "Tell me."

The Brother glanced at Tom and the others and whispered, "It's sensitive information."

The Master snatched the paper from the Brother's hands and unfolded it. The impatient scowl on his face was wiped away.

"Are you sure?"

"Yes, Sir," replied the Brother.

"You were right to interrupt me with this information. Prepare the troops," said The Master, dismissing the man with a wave of his hand.

Though The Master was no longer looking at him, the Brother bowed to his Master. When he rose, the Brother locked eyes with Tom and winked. He turned and crossed the ballroom at a much slower pace than when he had come in.

Tom wasn't sure what it meant. That had to have been Alistair, but he hadn't gotten a good look at his face. It wasn't until he felt the strange weight of his father's ring on his left pinky that he understood what had happened.

Fortunately, the news Brother Alistair had brought had perturbed The Master enough that he stood stock-still, his eyes trained on the piece of paper he held. He apparently had not yet realized the ring was no longer in his pocket, or that all four of Tom's friends wore identical Cheshire cat grins.

On his way out, Alistair had not only returned Tom's ring, but he'd also untied his friends without The Master noticing.

CHAPTER
TWENTY-EIGHT

ONCE ALISTAIR WAS out of the ballroom, he breathed a sigh of relief. He had accomplished his mission and made it out of the room alive. He hadn't appreciated being handled like a marionette by The Master and hoped there was a way to cleanse himself of the blood he'd ingested when this was all over.

He ran a hand over the brand on his arm. Perhaps he'd get a tattoo to cover it up.

For now, however, he needed to think fast. The Master expected him to prepare the troops for an imminent raid that wasn't coming. In hindsight, it may not have been the best idea. Then again, it was doubtful that The Master would leave the ballroom anytime soon, least of which to check that the orders he'd given to a trusted minion were being carried out. Having Tom and the focus on transferring were likely all-consuming at this point.

As he made his way back to his office, he wondered if a raid might be a good idea. No one at the MFO had asked for his location, though he was pretty sure they had triangulated his position from his phone. It was standard procedure for an undercover operative in the field.

If things went south, he would need an escape plan. That's how things usually worked, but this mission had been anything but typical.

Assuming Tom was able to neutralize The Master, someone would need to come in here, gather the minions, and ensure that they didn't carry out their leader's nefarious plans. They would need names and he could provide those. He'd be pegged as a whistleblower. Would his family be impacted?

What about Derek and his family? Alistair had kept tabs on Derek as best he could. It didn't appear that Derek has been assigned to any illegal activities. For the most part, Derek's job hadn't changed. He was already providing an invaluable service to the cause in the biochem lab. If the place was raided, he'd be ok. As would all the humans working at Vardo Ventures.

Alistair thought back to the lure he felt in being The Master's possible successor. Did The Master mean he could inherit Vardo Ventures? *Surely, he didn't mean Blood Magick*, Allistair wondered, thinking of Tom. Alistair pondered if that would at all be possible. Would there be a conflict of interest in an undercover agent inheriting a semi-legitimate shell company owned and operated by an evil Sorcerer? They were related after all...

If there wasn't any conflict, would Tom contest it? Though Tom's father had inherited the Estate when Brendan had allegedly died, any holdings that turned up once The Master's identity was revealed would technically go to Tom, John's heir, and now Custodian.

Regardless, an audit would need to be made to separate the legitimate activities from the fraudulent ones. They seemed to have done a fair job keeping things above board until now.

Alistair made it back to his office without running into anyone. He especially didn't want to meet Jameson. The boy gave him the creeps with his mangled face and his intense devotion to The Master. If there was ever one that fell into the Kool-Aid, it was him.

Alistair had investigated Jameson after their initial run-in. It was odd how jealous Jameson had become when finding out who Alistair was and the possibility that he might take his place as favorite minion, or even successor.

It turned out that he and Jameson were related as well. Brendan and Brian had a younger sister named Siobhan. She married and had five children. One of those children is Jameson's father, making them second cousins. Which also meant that he was Tom's second cousin as well. It was unclear if Jameson knew that when he attacked Tom at Harding Academy.

As the eldest by a few minutes, Brendan was the rightful heir. He inherited the Callahan family home, and he also became Custodian, which is why his children were Travelers, while Brian's were not.

From a young age, Brendan hadn't exhibited any magical abilities beyond Traveling, despite having a Witch for a mother. It was assumed that Brian had received the bulk of the magical gifts, so he wasn't sore when his brother became the heir. The brothers drifted apart when Brian left for Harding Academy, while Brendan headed for The Academy.

As for Siobhan, she married a powerful Warlock, and their children were among the strongest at Harding Academy. Liam, Jameson's father, was one of the co-conspirators currently serving time at The Hold for their involvement in the thefts and kidnappings.

Alistair was not at all surprised to find out that Jameson was the man's son. The apple never fell far from the tree.

Once he had secured his office, he texted the MFO for their input on how to proceed.

CHAPTER

TWENTY-NINE

THE MASTER WAS STILL STARING at the piece of paper Alistair had given him. Whatever it was, it had been an effective diversion.

Tom's mind raced. He had his ring back and his friends looked like they had a plan, which was good because he was drawing blanks.

Did they have enough information to strike? What was the end goal? Could they contain The Master until the CEMB could take him to The Hold? No. There was only one way out of this. The Master had to die. But how could they kill him without Tom becoming the new Blood Mage?

Maybe he should just go through with it, and they'd figure out a way to get it out of him safely later. Or perhaps once The Master died, Tom would be strong enough to wield the power safely. He could save his friends, heal the sick, wounded, and dying, and save the world!

The more he thought about it, the more the idea had merit. He didn't know what he'd been against it all this time. He was the Chosen One, after all. It should all go to him: the house, the Custodianship, and the power over life and death. It was his destiny. No. It was his legacy.

A few drops of his blood could end terrorism and put an end to famine. He would free humanity from its shackles.

"I'm ready, Sir. I'm ready to receive the gift."

The Master looked up then from the piece of paper, hope clear on his face.

"Are you really?"

From the corner of his eye, he could see Zaina's look of astonishment. He faced The Master.

"Yes. I understand now. The humans have lost their way. They need a new leader to ensure they no longer harm themselves," he said.

The Master's eyes grew wide, and his face contorted into what passed for a smile.

"You have the most impeccable timing," he said waving the paper. "This location is no longer secure; I say we take this to a safer venue."

Before Tom quite knew what he was doing, The Master pulled a Key from his pocket and a Door appeared.

"But...you... You said you couldn't Travel?" Tom stammered.

"I haven't had a Key in years, but I was able to retrieve my Key when I was home a few weeks ago. Remember when I took your Key? I needed it to open the Repository and retrieve my Key. The box will only open for the Custodian. As I had once been the Custodian and held your Key, it was easily fooled."

Tom thought back to that night. It had felt like The Master had his Key for mere minutes, but as history had shown, the Sorcerer had time to switch rings on Tom, surely, he'd have time to grab a Key from a box while Tom was fighting off the suit of armor.

The Master turned the knob and opened the Door, "Let's go, Tom. Our work here is done."

The Master held his arm out to Tom expectantly. Tom looked at his friends. Mandy was shaking her head.

"If we leave, your friends will be safe from both of us," said The Master.

It was exactly what Tom needed to hear and he moved forward.

CHAPTER
THIRTY

"NOW, BENNY!" screamed Mandy before Tom could cross the threshold.

Benny shot up, arms out, and yelled "Stop!"

The Master and Tom froze on the spot. The Master stood by the Door, pushing it open and Tom had stopped mid-stride, a few feet from The Master.

"Okay, guys we have 30 seconds what's the plan?" huffed Benny.

"Will they know they've been immobilized?" asked Zaina.

"No, they'll just hear me yelling stop, which is something I'd say to keep Tom from going through the Door, anyway," he replied.

"Okay, so if we need to, we can freeze them again," said Zaina, more to herself than to anyone else.

"I wouldn't press our luck," warned Arturo.

"I agree," said Mandy.

"I vote we take away Tom's ring. He might be faking it, but I don't think he's that good an actor."

"I agree. That was crazy talk. There's no way we're letting him keep the ring, let alone take the 'gift'. Hasn't he seen all the movies? It never ends well for the host. We need to end this parasite," Zaina sighed with haste.

Arturo was keeping time on his watch. "Fifteen seconds."

He moved closer to Tom and The Master. The Door was ajar, and he peeked in to see where they were going.

"I don't recognize the place, but it looks like someone's house. The psycho keeps referring to Tom's house as his home, odds are good that's where they're going. It's been empty since the attack."

"I could slip in and hide, maybe call Harding from the phone," suggested Mandy.

"Why don't we all go?" asked Benny.

"Don't you think they'd notice if we disappeared?" snapped Zaina.

Benny puffed out a sigh. "I guess."

"Everyone back to your places," cried Arturo.

They all scrambled back to their seats except for Benny, who stood with his hands in the air the way he had when he froze them.

The Door opened further, and Tom missed a step as he turned toward Benny.

"What?" he asked impatiently. Benny flinched. Already the ring was altering Tom's demeanor.

The Master's back was to them, and he didn't turn.

Benny stammered, "You can't go with him. You can't do this. This isn't you, Tom."

Tom looked at Benny with such disdain that even Mandy recoiled in her seat.

He lifted a hand and pushed the air as he said, "Sit down and shut up."

Benny was propelled back, and he fell into the chair with such force that it toppled backward.

With a satisfied nod, Tom faced The Master and headed for the door.

Meanwhile, Benny was scrambling to his feet, one hand on the fallen chair, and one in the air as he froze the pair again. When they stopped moving, he rested his forehead on the side of the chair.

"If he's faking it, he's doing a really good job of it," he said.

"Okay. Who has a better plan than me slipping in?" asked Mandy.

"Why should you go? Why not me or Arturo?" asked Zaina.

"Because I can freeze them if I need to. And they'll stay frozen for a lot longer than 30 seconds."

"Right," said Zaina, unconvinced.

"We need to stay here and face the minions. If no one comes for us, we'll need to get back to Harding on our own. Who else here knows how to drive?" asked Arturo.

"A car?" asked Benny. "You want to steal a car?"

"Got any better ideas?" asked Arturo. He checked his watch. "Fifteen seconds. I say Mandy goes, finds a phone, and calls Harding so they can come to get us. If no one comes after fifteen minutes, we break out of here."

"Agreed," said Zaina.

"I'm not ready. Freeze them again," said Mandy.

Arturo sighed and Benny sat awkwardly on the fallen chair until the evil duo resumed moving. When they did, he waved at them again.

"Go, they may start to notice something's off after three freezes," he said resting his head on the back of the chair.

There was less than a foot between Tom and the opening. Taking pains not to touch him, Mandy slipped in. It was the entryway of a house. Frantically, she searched for a quick hiding spot. She heard Arturo say 'fifteen seconds' and opted for the front closet. She highly doubted they would hang their robes there or need to retrieve a coat. She took a deep breath and exhaled as she waited for them to head for another room in the house.

"The study seems like the perfect spot, don't you think?" asked The Master.

"Yes, very fitting, Sir," replied Tom. Mandy heard their steps echoing down the hall away from her. She heard a door open then close again and dared to poke her head out. The coast was clear.

She eased out and closed the door noiselessly. She had two options. Either she went up the stairs and found a room with a phone, or she went through the sitting room and found the kitchen. If she went up, the stairs might creak and give her away. If she went to the kitchen, they might hear her through the wall. She opted for the living room, hoping she might find more rooms to choose from along the way.

She went through the sitting room, then the dining room until she reached the kitchen. Mercifully, the kitchen had doors, which she promptly closed. She searched for a phone and found the antique phone by the back wall, next to a door leading out onto the terrace. As she took the receiver, it occurred to her that she did not know the school's number.

She rarely called the school, and if she did, it was from her mobile. She checked the refrigerator; her mom always taped important numbers there. No luck. She checked the counter near the phone. It was clean and bare except for a phone message pad and a pen. She sighed in frustration.

Come on!

She tried the drawer and found a fancy notebook labeled 'Directory'.

Jackpot!

She opened the cover and there, on the first page, were emergency phone numbers, including one for Harding Academy. She dialed the number but got no response. It was after ten by now, no one would be answering the phones.

She checked the notebook. Surely someone as fancy as Mrs. Callahan would have a direct line to the Headmistress.

Bingo!

She prayed this would work. The phone rang once, twice, before someone picked up.

"Miss Clementine, it's Mandy. You need to hurry and come get the others at the castle. Tom and The Master have gone to Tom's house. I followed them here and I'm hiding in the kitchen," said Mandy in a single breath, as loud as she dared into the receiver.

"I can send Lady Mathilda immediately. She'll come to get you after she's retrieved them."

"Not just yet. They don't know I'm here. I'll be careful and report back if anything happens, I promise. I think we need to let them battle it out," she said.

"All right, dear. Please call back in ten minutes. If I don't hear from you, I'm sending Lady Mathilda. Please be careful dear." The old woman couldn't hide her concern for these kids dealing with problems beyond their paygrade.

"Okay. I should hang up now," said Mandy and replaced the receiver before the Headmistress could offer any more advice or admonitions.

Mandy had a plan and she only had ten minutes.

CHAPTER
THIRTY-ONE

"TELL me how this all started. I mean, I've figured out it started with Conor. Did you fake your own death? Did you body-snatch your own son?" asked Tom when they'd settled in the study.

The Master sat behind the desk. While Tom had felt odd sitting behind his dad's desk, it was even weirder to see The Master seated there. He had removed his robes upon entering, hanging them on the hook behind the door, nonchalantly, like he'd done it a million times.

If he'd been embodying each of Tom's ancestors for hundreds of years, it was fair to say that this was *his* study more than anyone else's. Would he have found more than his father's journals hidden around the room if Tom had taken the time?

Tom took in the man before him, for all intents and purposes this was his grandfather, Brendan, whom he didn't remember. He didn't look like anyone's grandad. He looked like death warmed over.

He was the embodiment of the consequences of Necromancy. You could bring people back to life, but did the person's soul come back into the body with them?

The Master looked to the fireplace, lost in thought for a moment, and began.

"It was a difficult birth. By all accounts, Conor should have died.

He came too soon and was so very frail and fragile. I should have let him die, but I breathed life into his tiny lungs and the answering wail stole my heart.

I loved Petunia, Brady, and Ian, but at that moment, I loved none so much as I loved Conor. I felt connected to him in a way I had never been to another in my life, not even my mother.

A few days after his birth, I awoke to the sounds of choking. In an instant, I had him over my arm, clapping his back to dislodge whatever was obstructing his airways. He stopped coughing so I turned him over and cradled him. I sat in the rocking chair, relieved that the crisis had passed only to realize that the reason he had stopped coughing was that he was no longer breathing. I pushed his tiny chest and puffed air into his mouth. It wasn't working. I did it again and again, and he still wouldn't breathe on his own though I could still feel a faint heartbeat. I continued to breathe for him, praying to every deity I could think of. I even called out to Lucifer himself. I'd have struck any bargain to bring him back.

That's when I heard them," he paused.

Tom, enthralled by the tale spoke up, "Who?"

The Master looked at Tom, made eye contact, and said "The Witches."

The Witches? What Witches?

Then Tom understood. "The ones you killed?"

"Yes. All of them. They leeched out of me and filled the room. The ghostly apparitions seemed to solidify as they took root on the earthly plane, pointing an accusatory finger at me. Only one of them spoke, the one who cursed me.

"You have broken the curse. Is this the product of your union with the Witch?" she said, pointing at the dead infant in my arms.

"Yes, they all are," I replied, looking to Brady and Ian behind me, asleep in their beds.

"Would you give your life in exchange for his?" she asked.

"Yes, yes, I would. Can you save him?"

"Your death will free us all; we are prepared to grant you this boon," she declared.

The Witches gathered in a tight circle around us and held hands. There were so many of them that they gathered in multiple outer circles around the first one.

The Witches spoke in a language I did not understand though I was a learned scholar. I continued to breathe for Conor regularly until I felt myself leave my body. From above, I could see Conor's chest rise and fall and the rosy hue that had come back into his cheeks.

The Witches started to leave. They didn't return to my body or use the door. They merely rose up, turning to mist before they hit the ceiling. The Witch who cursed me held out her hand to me, "Come, it's time to go."

I nodded and made to follow her. We both lifted off the ground, but just as she turned to mist, I held back and looked back at my child. I floated down to him one more time, meaning to gaze upon his sweet face but as I came close, he inhaled sharply, and.... breathed me in!"

THIRTY-TWO

MANDY SAT and cleared her mind. She needed to know the lay of the land and what was going on in that room before she executed her plan. In seconds, she was in astral form, flying through the house and poking her head into every room until she found them.

She listened to The Master's tale in fascinated horror.

Tom asked, "Is that how it works, The Blood Mage dies, and his essence leaves the body, floats around until someone breathes it in?"

"Yes," answered The Master.

"You, Brön, see it happening because you are out of your body. But does the host know it's happening? Can they see it?" asked Tom.

"I don't think so. I think it's like being in astral form, or a ghost. The spirit or essence is invisible to the human eye," replied The Master.

"So, the only clue we have that it worked is that the previous host dies and doesn't revive," said Tom.

"That is correct."

"And how are you planning to die, exactly?" asked Tom.

The Master smiled. "Besides your father, none of my hosts have had to resort to murder. No, I have a potion that will do the trick quickly and painlessly."

He pulled a vial from his pocket and placed it on the desk. The murky liquid had a purplish-black hue. All that was missing was a skull and crossbones to label it as poison.

Mandy took this as her cue. She flew back into her body in the kitchen, woke herself up, and crept back to the study. Tom was speaking, that was good. She took a deep breath and burst through the door.

Both men looked at her in surprise and she moved quickly before they could react. She froze them at full force. She could control the freezing level. Full force was lethal, it started at the extremities and made its way in. If it reached the organs, the subject died. She had to hurry.

She ran to Tom first, removed the ring and slipped it into her pocket. Then she grabbed the vial, uncorked it, and sped around the desk to The Master. She turned the rolling chair and tilted it back as far as it would and poured the potion into The Master's mouth. Once it was all in, she slowly eased him back into an upright position. Hopefully, he wouldn't choke on it, but if he died choking on his own poison, that was fine by her.

She pushed the chair away from the desk and further into the room, as far away from Tom as she could get it.

She unfroze Tom but refroze his feet so he couldn't move any closer and did the same to The Master, praying her plan would work.

The Master coughed as the liquid thawed and went down his throat. His eyes were huge as he realized what had just happened.

"*What have you done!?*" he croaked at Mandy, looming over him.

Tom screamed at her. "Get away from him! You can't be the host, you'll die."

"That's a risk I'm willing to take," she replied as they watched The Master's head loll and drop to his chest.

She didn't see anything happen, but she felt it. It was the smell that tipped her off, like a candle had just been extinguished, the smell of smoke filled her nostrils. She breathed in deeply to ensure she took in the 'gift' and coughed like someone taking the first drag of a cigarette. She breathed in again in case she had let the bugger escape by coughing.

That's when she felt it, felt *him*. He was angry with her, she could tell. She felt all at once revolted, nauseous and livid. She had him.

She froze The Master's body at full force to ensure it would no longer be a viable host and to ensure he was good and dead. She turned to Tom and unfroze him.

"The others will be here soon," she said before freezing herself at half-strength.

"Mandy, I don't know the spell to undo this!" exclaimed Tom rushing to stop her.

Before her mouth immobilized, she replied, "I know."

CHAPTER
THIRTY-THREE

TOM WAS DEBATING whether to leave Mandy while he took a Door back to Harding or try to carry her across the threshold. She wasn't frozen solid like a block of ice, only immobilized and cold to the touch. Her eyes were closed, but Tom saw she was breathing in and out regularly.

The Master, for his part, was frozen over completely, along with the chair he sat in. Tom wondered if he would thaw out if he were rolled in front of the fireplace, had there been a fire.

He was interrupted in his musings by a Portal. Lady Mathilda came out, a frantic look in her eyes, anticipating the worst. She took in the scene and turned a questioning gaze to Tom.

"The Master's dead. Mandy's the host and she's frozen herself to save me," he said in a single breath.

Lady Mathilda strode over to Mandy, picked her up, and went through the Portal.

Tom sighed with relief and took out his Key. He thought of going back to the castle to check on his friends but remembered he couldn't open a Door inside the castle. If Lady Mathilda had known to come to his house, it likely meant his friends were back at Harding.

Tom's Door opened outside the main entrance. He really hoped the main door was unlocked or that there was a night butler on duty.

He tried the handle and rang the bell when it didn't budge. He rang it three times for good measure. He had barely removed his hand from the bell when the door was yanked open by the same ancient butler as usual.

"Once is quite enough," he said as he stepped aside to let Tom in, disdain dripping from his every feature.

"I'm sorry, it's an emergency," yelled back Tom as he ran to Miss Clementine's office.

He knocked but got no answer. This knob turned easily, but Tom found the room empty.

Where are they?

He thought for a moment and deduced they might have taken Mandy to the infirmary and tried to remember where that was. It was near the cafeteria, he recalled and started walking in that direction.

The halls were quiet, it was after ten. All the other students were in bed. Tom turned left when he got to the cafeteria since turning right led to the sports amphitheater. He jogged down the hall until he found a door marked 'Infirmary'.

He sagged in relief when he found the door not only unlocked but ajar and heard voices within. He pushed open the door and followed the sound. Whoever it was, they were arguing.

Once he got closer, he recognized Zaina's angry tones.

"If you unfreeze her, she'll probably die because she can't handle the Blood Magick. Then, that 'thing' will float out of her and pop into the next person and so on until it takes root, or everyone is dead."

"But The Master said if there's no one else available, the spirit will go back into their original body and revive it. The Master's dead and nowhere near here. Do you think it will find it and jump back in?" asked Arturo.

"No, Mandy's frozen him completely. There's no coming back from that. We could incinerate his body to be certain, though," replied Professor Hilltop.

"Yes, do that now before anything else is decided," interjected Tom as he walked into the room where they were all assembled around Mandy's frozen form.

"Tom!" friend Benny. "I'm so glad you're okay."

Tom gave his friend a curt nod.

"What were you thinking?" he said, shooting Benny, Arturo, and Zaina a disgusted look.

"Why couldn't you let me handle it. Now look what happened," he said, his voice cracking as he pointed to Mandy.

"I'm sure we can figure out how to save Mandy, Tom," said Professor Montague in a soothing tone.

"What if you can't, what if she dies, and more people die. This was *my* responsibility," he said, poking a hard finger at his chest.

"There was no way we were letting that thing take over your body. You had the ring for less than a minute and already you thought the psycho's plans sounded pretty good. No one should have that kind of power, not even the kindest, most well-intentioned soul. Mandy did what any of us would have done to save you, to save us all, from that fate," said Zaina.

Tom knew she was right, but he felt so powerless. If he had his ring...

My ring!

"Mandy took my ring, it must be in one of her pockets," he said, taking a step forward.

Professor Hilltop clapped an iron hand around Tom's arm, "Let it go, Tom. Blood Magick is what got us into this mess, it's certainly not the answer now."

He didn't let go of Tom's arm, though he relaxed his grip.

"Yes, Sir. You're right. What do we do now?" he asked, relaxing a bit to show the teacher he wasn't about to jump on Mandy in search of his ring.

Professor Hilltop gave Tom an assessing gaze and let go of him. He stayed close, just in case.

Miss Clementine took the phone receiver from the nurse's desk and dialed a number.

"Burn the body, and the ring too," she said to whoever was at the other end. "And have them look for any other similar rings in The Master's quarters at the castle and burn those too. She confirmed the order and hung up.

The room was silent for a moment.

Zaina cleared her throat and squared her shoulders. "The truth is, Mandy's already breathed in the spirit. The only reason she's not dead yet is because she's put herself in some kind of stasis. Let's not pretend she's getting out of this alive."

Benny started to cry, as did Miss Clementine.

"Can't the High Elves save her? Can't they perform an exorcism?" asked Tom desperately, looking at Lady Mathilda through tear-filled eyes.

"I'm afraid not. She would come out of stasis as soon as she reached The Summer Isles, and we might not have enough time to do much of anything. Earthly magic cannot cross the barrier," replied Lady Mathilda.

"I'm sorry to be the one to say this, but the only course of action is to place Mandy in an airtight, magically sealed chamber to ensure the spirit cannot escape," said Professor Hilltop.

"But won't she slowly die from the freezing spell?" asked Miss Clementine, dabbing at her eyes.

"We can reverse the spell once she's inside," suggested Professor Montague.

"So, she'd be in a glass prison?" asked Benny, incredulous.

"No, Benny, we'd put her to sleep until we can figure out how to separate her from the spirit," replied Professor Hilltop.

"Won't the Blood Magick kill her then?" asked Tom.

"Yes, but with nowhere to go, it will have to revive her in order to stay alive."

"She'll be a zombie. Even if we can remove the spirit later, Mandy as we know her will be gone!" cried Benny.

"Poor Mandy, what has she gotten herself into?" asked Tom.

"I'm afraid Mandy knew exactly what she was getting into," replied Miss Clementine.

"When I spoke to her over the phone, she seemed determined to see this through."

"Yeah, she was adamant that she should be the one to sneak into your house while you and The Master were immobilized. Sorry, Tom, but I think this was her plan all along."

"I have to agree with Zaina," put in Arturo. "When Benny and I were on the astral plane trying to figure out how to get ourselves out of there, she joined us. She was the one who suggested Benny freeze you so we could coordinate."

"We hadn't anticipated the Door thing. I think Mandy had planned to do exactly what she did but back there at the castle," said Benny shaking his head in disbelief as he said the words.

"So, what do we do? How do we decide?" Tom asked, tears streaming down his cheeks.

Miss Clementine cleared her throat. "We don't, dear. Her parents will."

She turned to Lady Mathilda as she wiped the tears from her face, checked that her chignon was still in place, and smoothed down her skirt.

"Shall we?" she asked the High Elf.

Before leaving, she turned to those assembled and said, "I believe the family would appreciate some privacy when they arrive. You should all go to bed. There is nothing more to be done tonight. Professors Montague and Hilltop will watch over her until we return. Then, they too will retire."

She spoke with her sternest Headmistress voice. It wasn't a suggestion; it was an order.

Tom, Zaina, Benny, and Arturo approached Mandy in turn and spoke their goodbyes. It was the last time they would see her alive.

CHAPTER
THIRTY-FOUR

Tom, Zaina, Benny, and Arturo reluctantly made their way to the dorms. When they reached the outer door, Arturo hesitated. He looked like he wanted to say something but seemed to reconsider and said goodnight before walking down the hall to his room.

The others stood outside for a while longer, knowing they couldn't talk once they went into the common room.

"I'm so tired, but I don't know if I'll be able to sleep not knowing what will happen to Mandy," said Benny, resting his head on the wall. He looked like he was about to keel over.

"I know what you mean. I keep thinking about her poor parents. I wish I could go home and hug my mom," said Zaina. All the fight had drained out of her. She suddenly looked so vulnerable, that it made Tom's heart break all over again.

He'd been so happy to have found these new friends but to look at them now. Arturo had looked so sad, too shell-shocked to admit he didn't want to be alone. Benny was traumatized and looked like may never be cheerful again. And Zaina, the fearless Amazon, wanted nothing more than to curl into bed with her mom.

Who would Tom turn to? His mom? His sister? No, there was no way he was going to them with this news. As much as he would have liked some comfort, he knew that wasn't an option.

"Can't you use a token to go home?" asked Tom.

"They only work on weekends, and I don't think the teachers are up to dealing with a special request," she replied.

"I could take you. With a Door I mean," he suggested. He turned to Benny and said, "I can take you too if you want to be with your family."

Benny looked so grateful when he replied. "That would be great, man. You're sure it's no trouble?"

"Not at all, but I think we should let Arturo know we're leaving so he can tell the teachers in the morning. Unless you plan to be back before breakfast. Do you have tokens to come back, or do I need to come pick you up?"

Benny looked down at his feet and said, "I have a token, but I don't think I'll be back in the morning. There's no happy ending to this story and I'm not up to dealing with the fallout, let alone going to class as if nothing happened. I might take a few days to process."

Tom patted him on the shoulder. "It's okay Benny, I get it. Why don't I get you home while Zaina goes to square things with Arturo? I'll be back for her next."

Benny nodded. So did Zaina. She was halfway down the hall when Tom added, "Do you mind meeting me outside the front entrance, I don't want to deal with the butler again."

She frowned but gave him a thumbs up.

Tom pulled out his Key and looked at Benny. "I think you said you lived in Richmond, London, right?" asked Tom.

"You remembered!" replied Benny, clearly impressed that Tom had paid attention.

"I'm going to need an address, Benny."

CHAPTER

THIRTY-FIVE

THE TRIP to London had been short and uneventful. It was past two a.m. and Tom dropped Benny off in front of his house without being seen. Despite the late hour, there were lights on in the house. Benny hugged Tom, thanked him again for the ride, and promised to be in touch in a few days.

When Tom went back to school, Zaina was waiting with Arturo.

"He didn't want to be alone either," said Zaina.

"Got room for one more in the cab?" joked Arturo.

"Sure, the more the merrier. Where to next?" Tom asked.

Zaina and Arturo looked at each other and shrugged.

"Zaina, are you going to Glasglow?" asked Tom.

Zaina shuffled her feet and replied, "No. Actually, do you mind dropping me off at my nanna's home? My mom is there visiting. I was supposed to go there this weekend, but now is as good a time as any."

"No worries, just give me an address. Arturo, do you want to tag along or wait here?" said Tom.

Arturo looked around at his dark surroundings and said he'd go along.

Zaina gave him an address, and they were hit with the warm, coastal air of Sidon, Lebanon. It was such a huge contrast to the frigid humidity of Northern Scotland that Tom was happy Arturo had come along. There was no way he was going back to Harding tonight.

Here too, the lights were on, and the front door opened moments after they arrived.

"Zaina, are you alright?" asked a woman who looked so much like Zaina it could only be her mother. She embraced her daughter, casting the same suspicious look at Tom and Arturo that Zaina often had.

"Yes, Mom. I'm fine. These are my friends from school Tom and Arturo. Tom is a Traveler, he gave me a ride," she said. She shook each boy's hand.

"There's a story here, but I think it can wait. Would the boys like to come in, and have a bite to eat?"

"Thank you, Mrs...uh, m'am, but I need to get Arturo home to his family," replied Tom.

Arturo spoke up. "Unless Tom is in a hurry to get home, I'd be willing to stay for a while."

Tom shook his head. "Nope."

"Then it's settled. You'll eat. You'll tell me what happened, and if you want, you can stay the night. Outside, of course," said Zaina's mom.

Both boys replied "Of course," in unison and laughed. It was a much-needed release from the tension of the day.

THEY HAD ARRIVED at the tail end of a late dinner. Zaina's grandmother and aunts sat around the table drinking wine and enjoying each other's company. All of them mothers, the women wanted to know what had brought the children back from school on a Tuesday in the middle of the night.

Zaina told the tale succinctly and concluded by saying none of them felt like talking about it. The women fussed over them, pushing treats and extra servings of everything until they were stuffed and sleepy.

Tom had never enjoyed a meal more than that one. Not only was the food delicious, but it most certainly hadn't come from a takeaway carton. But more than that, they had made him feel so welcome, so... enveloped. Like this was the safest place in the world and nothing bad could happen. He understood why Zaina wanted to come here, to her true home, not their flat in Glasglow.

Arabella was a decent parent, but she wasn't *this* kind of a mother. The kind that fed you, stroked your hair and wrapped you in a warm blanket or, in this case, rolled you into a handmade quilt on the back porch.

The women said goodnight, leaving the boys to sleep under the stars. It was surprisingly a lot more comfortable out in the open air. The stars were out, and they had the soothing lap of the ocean mere steps away.

"Thanks, Tom," said Arturo quietly. He hadn't spoken much at dinner and hadn't said a word since the ladies had said goodnight. Tom had assumed he'd fallen asleep.

"What for?" he asked.

"For agreeing to stay. I really didn't feel like going home."

"Why did you come then?" asked Tom, turning on his side to face Arturo.

"I didn't want to be alone, but I didn't really want to go home. People always expect Italian families to be cheerful, loud, and fun. Like Zaina's family. Mine's...not."

"Same, dude. Same."

Tom turned on his back and held out his fist to Arturo. He nodded at the returning fist bump and said, "Goodnight, buddy."

CHAPTER
THIRTY-SIX

MR. AND MRS. HONEYWELL, Mandy's parents, were understandably distraught. Professors Montague and Hilltop took their leave when they arrived, and Miss Clementine let them go through as many stages of grief as they needed to process what had happened to their daughter. It was difficult.

Unfortunately, it wasn't the first time she had to impart such catastrophic news to a student's parents. It happened rarely, but there had been deaths at Harding Academy for the Magical Arts over the years.

Lady Mathilda stayed with them. People tended to be calmer in the presence of a High Elf. Their regal stature and kind, benevolent faces were usually enough to curb even the angriest outburst, merited as it may be.

An hour later, they were sipping tea and trying to decide what was best. Lady Mathilda and Miss Clementine had stepped out for a few moments to let them discuss it in privacy.

When they returned, it was time to take action.

"The daughter you know, and love is gone. I understand it's hard to come to terms with this when she's standing right there looking like she might wake up at any moment. But I can assure you that if she were to wake up, it wouldn't be your daughter. She'd only be playing host to an evil incarnate," explained Miss Clementine. She knew they were religious people and used the term 'evil' to drive her point home.

"We understand," said Mr. Honeywell, his holding his wife's hand. He looked resigned; they both did. They had shed their tears, more would surely come later, but now was the time to be practical.

"We don't want our daughter's body, let alone her soul, to be defiled by that...that...that demon. We've agreed it's best if she and the beast are incinerated while she's still in the frozen state. I know it's technically murder, and I'm prepared to go to hell to save my baby's soul. She won't feel a thing. Heck, I'm surprised she's still alive after being frozen for so long."

"We've been monitoring her. She's given herself a half-freeze, knowing we'd need a few hours to figure things out," replied Miss Clementine.

Mrs. Honeywell dabbed at her eyes with a hand-embroidered handkerchief. "That's our Mandy, always saving the day. You know, she once saved an entire family of goats from a barn fire at our neighbor's house? She said she heard them bleating in the night and rushed out in her jammies to save them. She saved the whole family. If she hadn't rushed out screaming *fire*, we wouldn't have called the firefighters when we did. If we hadn't, the elderly couple next door may have slept through the fire and died," she said. "She was only ten!"

A fresh batch of tears sprung from every eye in the room.

"Yes, well, it seems Mandy was destined to be a heroine," concluded Lady Mathilda.

She poured some more tea and delicately broached the topic of having Mandy transported to a secure location.

"Would you like to oversee the transfer, or would you prefer to say your goodbyes here, now."

They looked at each other and nodded. They had discussed it. "We've already said our goodbyes. We'd like to be notified when she's... when it's over," replied Mr. Honeywell.

"What will we tell people?" asked Miss Clementine. "The students, the other parents, they'll want to know."

"We'd like the truth to be known in the magical community. Her sacrifice needs to be recognized. As for the human world, we'll say she was mauled by a bear while hiking in the woods. People will believe that since we do a lot of hiking. It's descriptive enough that they won't ask too many questions, nor will they ask why it's a closed coffin when we have the funeral."

"Very well. We'll be holding a ceremony in her honor here at school later this week and we'll make sure everyone understands the critical role she played in The Master's undoing," replied Miss Clementine.

"Would you like a few more minutes with your daughter before I take you back?" asked Lady Mathilda.

"No, we should let you get on with it," said Mr. Honeywell though both parents stopped to give their daughter a kiss and an awkward hug before they left.

After they'd gone, Miss Clementine called the CEMB and asked them to take over.

She sat next to Mandy, waiting for the team of specialists, and cried.

CHAPTER

THIRTY-SEVEN

THE NEXT MORNING, neither Tom nor Arturo felt like going back to school, but they wanted to know what was going on. Tom knew he would need to call his mom before Miss Clementine did since they were already late for class.

When his mum picked up the phone, he knew immediately that the Headmistress had beaten him to it.

Arabella was livid.

"Why didn't you call me? Why didn't you come home? The entire magical community is up in arms about this!" she yelled into the phone.

"What do you mean?" asked Tom. It hadn't been twelve hours.

"The CEMB raided The Master's castle last night. They've got the whole place on lock-down. No one goes in or out until everyone's been questioned and cleared."

Wow, that was fast. That must be Alistair's doing. He must have gotten busy as soon as he knew they were safely away from the castle.

"What else are they saying?" he asked. This was perfect. He wouldn't need to go to school to get the lowdown. His mom was such a gossip, she'd know everything before the reporters did.

"They're saying it was a young girl who saved the day. Who saved *you* from turning into the next monster? I can't imagine what her parents are going through, but I'll be sure to thank them somehow as soon as I find an appropriate way to do so," she stammered.

"Mam, where do you get this stuff?" asked Tom, amazed at the details.

"Well, some I heard through the grapevine. Some I heard from Miss Clementine when she called to let me know that you were safe but apparently *missing*," her words grew louder and louder until Tom had to hold the receiver away from his ear. Arturo, sitting nearby chuckled and Tom mouthed 'you're next' while he pointed at his friend.

"I'm sorry, Mam. I meant to come home last night. But I was giving my friends a lift, and it was so late that Zaina's mom insisted we crash here for the night. I should have at least called, but I didn't want to worry you in the middle of the night," he said, hoping the logic of his explanation would pacify his mother.

Though he didn't doubt that Arabella had been genuinely worried when learning he was missing, he was pretty sure she felt worse for not knowing where her son was when Miss Clementine called. It made her look bad.

"You still haven't told me where you are," she replied, apparently prepared to accept his explanation at face value.

"I'm with Arturo at Zaina's grandmother's house," he replied. He didn't want his mom to get any ideas, let alone ask more questions than she already had.

"Tom Callahan, you try my patience. Where. Are. You?"

"Oh, right. I'm in Lebanon. Specifically in Sidon, by the ocean. It's beautiful here," he said.

"Well, when you've thanked your hostess and are done with your little holiday at the beach, I want you to come home if you're not planning on attending classes today. You have one hour," she stated.

"Um, okay. But when you say home, which home do you mean?" Tom asked, genuinely confused.

"Don't be fresh with me, young man. I mean home to Cork, of course. Now that the threat is gone, it's time to get back to life as usual," she said and promptly hung up.

Tom looked at the phone in disbelief. "If I hung up on her, I'd be grounded for a month.

Life as usual?

She, Tabitha, and everyone else would resume their busy social lives as if nothing had happened. But for Tom, his friends, and Mandy's parents, life would never be the same.

He motioned for Arturo that the phone was free for him to use.

"My mom's giving me an hour, so we need to wrap things up and get moving," he said.

Arturo nodded and called his family.

TOM FOUND Zaina out on the back deck, lying in the morning sun in a bikini. He tried to avert his eyes, but she was so hot he had trouble forming a coherent thought. Sensing his presence, or perhaps his ogling, she opened her eyes and looked at him.

"Do you want to go swimming? I'm sure I can find a pair of shorts to fit you and Arturo," she said, shading the sun from her eyes with her hand.

"It will have to be a quick dip. I just spoke to my mom, and she wants me home ASAP," he replied.

"Yeah, sure, no problem. Hold on and I'll get those shorts."

She got up and Tom swore she took her sweet time sashaying back into the house because she knew he was checking out her butt. Tom slapped himself.

Stop lusting after your friend's assets, you perve! Remember Lola, your girlfriend?

Lola! He missed her something fierce. That's who he wanted to see last night, but he couldn't just open a Door to The Academy on a Tuesday night with no warning. And she would have been even more worried than his mom if he'd sent a Traveling letter. Chances were she wouldn't have gotten it until morning anyway because it had been after lights out.

Though he was sure the Headmaster and staff would know what happened, he doubted anyone at The Academy, including Lola and Devlin, would have a clue. It was better for everyone if they found out later. He would send her a quick note to check-in since he hadn't had a chance last night and he'd tell her and Devlin everything on the weekend.

Arturo came out with Zaina, already clad in ridiculous, Hawaiian-type swim shorts. He made a convincing runway turn and Tom burst out laughing. Zaina threw an even more hideous pair in his face.

"They were my grandpa's," she said with a scowl.

The boys stopped laughing and Tom went inside to change.

They stayed for more than an hour. Morning was the best time to be outside in this part of the world since it got so hot by mid-day. It was also why people ate so late at night, after the heat of the day had burned off.

They dried off, had another meal, and thanked their hostesses profusely. They both had a standing invitation any time they wanted to come back.

Zaina hugged them before they left. At their identical looks of surprise, she merely replied, "If you tell anyone, I'll break your fingers."

She was serious, but after a beat, they all started laughing.

"I'll see you at school in a few days," she said as they left.

CHAPTER

THIRTY-EIGHT

TOM STOOD in his father's study, his study, and stared at where The Master had sat frozen in front of the fireplace. Both the man and the chair had been removed, and Tom mourned the loss of both.

The man had been his grandfather, after all. He would have liked to know him before he'd been possessed by Brön. When had it happened? When he was an infant like Conor, or later in life like his father?

Tom mourned the chair too. He'd loved how the chair held the imprint of his father's form, how it felt like a hug from his father every time he sat in it. He remembered how he'd sat on his father's lap, pretending to write important papers, sealing them in wax.

Tom mourned his father's ring. That, too, was gone forever. Although now that he knew the ring's history, he thought he might find another trinket to remember his father by.

He didn't really need a memento. The whole study was a reminder of his father, as were the many journals he'd take the time to find and read whenever he came home from school.

School. There was another topic that needed to be addressed. Without the ring, Tom had no gift beyond his ability to Travel and cast spells. He could continue at Harding. Not everyone at Harding had special abilities and all were still considered Witches and Warlocks.

Miss Clementine had called to let him know about the memorial for Mandy on Friday and to request that he be in attendance. After he had promised to be there, she had broached the topic, knowing Tom would be feeling ambivalent once more about his future at Harding. She was right. It had taken him a long time to choose Harding when he had special abilities, but now that he was basically just a Traveler, he wondered where he fit.

"I'd like to think about it over the weekend. I'll be at school at the memorial on Friday, but I don't feel up to attending classes just yet."

"I understand, Tom. Take your time. We'll be here when you're ready," the Headmistress replied.

Tom jumped when he felt a hand on his shoulder.

"I miss him too," his mom said, assuming Tom was thinking about his father. He placed a hand over hers and squeezed.

He'd been vague with the details of what had happened in the study, afraid his mom would freak out, and decide to redecorate the room to exorcise it from The Master's presence. She couldn't equate The Master with the man her father-in-law had been. To her, the man had died and whoever came back was a changeling.

Tom was glad she hadn't wanted to talk about his experience ad nauseam. It's what made it bearable to stay home these last few days as that's what would have happened at school. People would want to know everything.

He texted Arturo, Zaina, and Benny a few times to see how they were. He'd even offered to go and get them to hang out wherever they wanted, but everyone still needed to process Mandy's death in their own way.

For Tom, it was a visit to her parents in Vermont. His mom had advised against it, but he felt compelled to go anyway. It was his fault after all.

TOM STOOD outside the Honeywell home. Tom had never been to this part of America before. It was so pretty, surely the wary settlers could have come up with a better name than New England.

Mandy had often spoken of her home in Vermont, of skiing and hiking, and the joy she and her family felt from being outside together, in all kinds of weather.

It was early Spring now. Mandy would miss the new flowers blooming, the kittens, puppies, ducklings, and foals being born. But Tom was here to witness it on her behalf, and he would tell her parents the tale as it had happened. They deserved to know all of it. And the teachers didn't know the half of it.

He took a deep breath and rang their doorbell. He waited, rocking on the ball of his feet, telling himself that it was going to be alright. If they yelled at him, hated him, or even struck him, it was their right, and perhaps they would all feel better.

The door opened and a girl of about fifteen stared back at him with Mandy's eyes. Her sister, Jessica. Jessie. Tom hadn't counted on her being home, but of course, she wouldn't be at school days after her sister's murder.

"Hi, you must be Jessie. I'm..." he started.

"Tom," she said simply and moved aside to let him in.

He entered and she closed the door. They stood awkwardly in the entrance.

"I'm.... I'm sorry," he said, trying to put as much emotion and sincerity behind those horribly inadequate words.

"Thanks. I guess you're here to see my parents," she replied, and Tom nodded.

"Would you like to see her room before you go out to see them? They're out back."

Tom wondered about the appropriateness of visiting Mandy's room. They hadn't been close friends. No, that wasn't right. They hadn't known each other long, but they had become close in their short time as part of a growing friendship. The Four Musketeers, one of them had said. If he'd hung out with Mandy at her home, he'd have seen her room, her stuff, her inner sanctum. The fact that Jessie wanted to show him Mandy's room also counted for something. It meant that Mandy had spoken of him at home, that he wasn't a complete stranger. It could also mean that Jessie needed to share the memory of her sister with someone who knew another part of her, as though combining their knowledge would make her whole again, if only for a moment.

"I'd love that," he replied, and Jessie led the way.

It was a large, modern house, full of light. Every room he walked by had floor-to-ceiling windows and simple yet elegant furnishings. From the outside, it had looked like there were two-stories, but now, he saw it was an illusion. The ceiling was over eight feet high, everywhere, and for a moment he wondered if one of her parents was a High Elf, for surely, they would feel at home here.

He couldn't imagine how Mandy and Jessie could stand going to school in a dark, damp, and gloomy castle in Scotland when they lived in such an airy, luminous, and warm space.

Once they'd passed the common areas, they veered to the right toward what Tom thought might be the kid's wing. Mandy's was the one on the end. Her room was shaped like a rhombus, all windows, and odd angles.

Her bed sat against the only windowless wall. The decor was as sunny and bubbly as Mandy herself. There would be no comparing versions today. Mandy had been her authentic self with everyone. Cheerful, optimistic, and fiercely loyal.

Tom trailed a hand along her vanity table where colorful baubles and fruity scents awaited her return. Her desk was stacked with biochem manuals. On a shelf above it were numerous models of atoms, or whatever the spheres and sticks were meant to represent.

He walked over to her bookcase and looked at the books that Mandy read for fun. It was mostly science fiction with a few thrillers thrown in here and there. Tom sank into the bright yellow beanbag and picked up the one she'd been reading.

He opened it to the bookmarked page and started reading. He'd read a paragraph before remembering that Jessie was in the room with him. When he looked up, it wasn't Jessie he saw but her parents, standing in the doorway, looking at him.

He scrambled to his feet, replaced the bookmark, and bent down to place the book exactly where he'd found it. He even tried to put the beanbag back to the way it had been, but it was a futile endeavor.

He wiped his hands on his jeans and said those lame words again. "I'm so sorry."

"Jessica told us you were here. We're glad you came," said Mrs. Honeywell, her face calm, patient, understanding.

Tom stood, rooted to the spot, unable to speak as tears suddenly sprung to his eyes. He opened his mouth to say something, anything that might make things right, but the lump in his throat was choking him.

Tom hadn't cried. He hadn't let himself cry because he didn't feel like he deserved to cry when other people had lost so much. Because of him and his psycho family, these people had lost a daughter. And the world had been robbed of one of the most exceptional human beings who had ever lived.

The floodgates had opened now, here of all places, and shame crept up his cheeks before sinking down to his heart to blend with the guilt he already felt. Try as he might, he just couldn't stop crying.

Mrs. Honeywell came into the room and wrapped Tom into a hug. At first, he just stood there lamely, arms hanging, feeling like such a coward. When Mrs. Honeywell started stroking the back of his hair and whispering, "It's okay. It's okay. You're going to be alright," in soothing tones as she rocked him back and forth in her arms, Tom lost it completely.

Ugly, retched sobs wracked his body and he clung to her. He clung to her because he needed an anchor. He needed a mother, someone to take his side. But then he clung to her because she was Mandy's mother. These arms had held Mandy. This woman's kindness had made Mandy into the kind and generous person she had been. Through her, he clung to Mandy.

When his sobs subsided, he held on, because he understood that he too was a proxy for Mandy. He took a deep breath and released the heaviness that had weighed him down. He had come here expecting anger and recriminations. Instead, he had found solace.

CHAPTER
THIRTY-NINE

AFTER HIS CRYING WAS OVER, and he apologized for his embarrassing and inappropriate display, he sat with the Honeywells on their patio. He told them everything. From his first day at school where Mandy had shown him around, to the last moments they had spent together in his father's study.

They told him about her childhood, her magical abilities, her dreams for the future, and about how she'd had a crush on him since the first day he'd arrived at Harding.

He hadn't known. He thought she was just being friendly. By that token, he might have to assume that Zaina had a crush on him because they'd both reacted pretty much the same way when they found out he was transferring to Harding. He didn't know how to feel about that.

When the conversation started to die down, he thanked them for their hospitality and their generosity. It had been a cathartic day for all of them and he was glad he came.

HE WENT to school the next day. It was Mandy's memorial. It was the first day back for Benny and Zaina as well. Arturo had gone back the day before.

As they took their seats in the assembly room, Tom spied Jessica in the front pew with her parents. She gave him an encouraging wave and then turned back to face the podium where Miss Clementine was about to address the room.

Though she spoke eloquently, all eyes were on the larger-than-life portrait of a smiling, windswept Mandy, arms extended in triumph on the summit of Mount Washington.

Tom had never hiked a day in his life, but he wanted to go to New Hampshire and walk in Mandy's footsteps until he reached the top of the mountain. Would she be there? Would he feel as carefree and joyful as the Mandy in the picture did?

Once Miss Clementine had concluded her speech, she called Mandy's parents to the podium. Only Mr. Honeywell rose. Tom spoke of Mandy's values, conviction, and ultimate courage and his parting words were met with a standing moment of silence.

Next was Jessica, who spoke about the bond between sisters, but also the sisterhood she's found here at school and that everyone should find comfort in friendship. If those attending hadn't been moved by the two previous speakers, they were bound to be a puddle of tears after Jessie's speech.

A few of the other friends told amusing stories and anecdotes to lighten the mood, but when it was over, and the parting song started to play over the loudspeakers, there wasn't a dry eye in the house.

```
"Ain't no sunshine when she'd gone.
 It's not warm when she's away..."
```

CHAPTER

FORTY

ALISTAIR HAD NEVER BEEN SO tired in his life. Less than an hour after sending his text to the MFO, the castle was stormed by an army of magical operatives who quickly shut the place down.

Alistair had provided access to all personal records, and a coordinated task force was also dropping on all Vardo employees or Brothers who were not residing at the castle.

Everyone was detained and questioned extensively.

Though he wasn't heading up the investigation, Alistair was their man on the inside and his input was required throughout the grueling process of separating the guilty from the innocent.

He was up all night, drafting supplementary non-disclosure agreements and compensation packages for the employees wanting to leave Vardo following the events that had transpired.

He was asked to step in as acting Director General. Not because he was related to Brendan Callahan or had any right to the company, but because he was the only person that they could trust to oversee the legitimate side of things while they untangled the rest of it. It would take more than one night to get to the bottom of The Master's web of deception.

For the most part, Vardo employees were regular humans hired for the jobs that were written in their HR files.

Not all Brothers were Vardo employees and some of them had been hard to locate once they'd been identified by their brethren.

When he finally got home, he found Derek in their suite of rooms. Seated on the couch, he didn't look like he'd slept at all either. It was apparent that he'd been waiting for his return.

Derek had been cleared after his first round of questioning, but Kenya had not. She had been taken in for further questioning by the MFO. The fact that Derek was in the room could have as much been the fact that he wanted answers than the fact that he had nowhere else to go.

Though all he wanted was to sink into oblivion, Alistair walked over to the opposite couch and sat. He was about to speak when Derek put a hand up to stop him.

"Have you known from the start?" he asked. The angry set of his jaw was a sure indication of the direction this conversation was going.

Alistair nodded.

"Is that why you came to the funeral?"

"No, of course not! I went because we're mates and your da' died," he insisted.

"If we're such good mates, why have you been lying to me for weeks?" he asked, slapping a hand on his lap.

This was why Alistair didn't have close relationships. Those he got close to inevitably found out he'd been lying to them. Sometimes it was small things like his real name. But other times, it was massive like he was working undercover to catch an evil Sorcerer and had used a mate to achieve his goals.

Regardless of the size or breadth of the lies, the issue was always that he lied. He had broken trust. It invalidated everything he and the person had shared. He was used to it, but it never got easy.

"I'm sorry I couldn't tell you. I know you won't believe me, but I've really enjoyed the time we've spent together since we met up again back home. Coming here and getting the job was as much an adventure for me as it was for you. I hope you can forgive the lies by omission that I was required to tell."

Derek's jaw clenched once and relaxed. Alistair could tell that he didn't want to stay angry. If it had been him, he'd have been disappointed and perhaps a little frightened.

"Kenya...they took her away. Do you know if she's being charged with anything?" he questioned.

"I'm not at liberty to say," Alistair replied and felt like a heel. "But I don't think her involvement will warrant a stay at The Hold if that's what you're worried about."

He could give his friend that peace of mind, at least.

"I mean, I really love her, but I only joined the Brotherhood because she urged me to do so and because I saw you going along with it. The whole thing never sat right with me and now I have to wonder if the relationship was all a sham," he said, putting his head in his hands.

"I really don't know what to tell you. It seemed like you two hit it off right from the start, but I'm in no position to judge someone's sincerity. She could have been a plant. Like me," replied Alistair, his voice barely above a whisper for that last bit.

They didn't speak for a few minutes and Alistair fought to stay awake. He owed it to his friend to answer all his questions.

"So, you knew that my dad was murdered by your cousin this whole time," said Derek. It wasn't a question, but neither was it an accusation. It was just a statement.

"Yes."

He didn't bother apologizing. As far as he was concerned, that's one secret Derek could have gone on not knowing. It served no purpose but to open wounds that had barely begun to heal.

The issuing silence was uncomfortable. Alistair finally asked what he really wanted to know.

"Are you staying at Vardo?"

Derek sat up and looked at him, lips pursed as though unsure how to answer.

"It's the best job I've ever had. I really love it here, but I don't know if I can stay, with all that's happened."

"Same," replied Alistair.

"What if I told you the headquarters would be moved to another facility, would you be interested then?" he continued.

Derek looked up at the ceiling and thought for a moment. "Would there be as many perks?"

"More! A state-of-the-art building, a campus, and modern, eco-friendly lodgings for those who want them," said Alistair.

Derek perked up, "Tell me more!"

"I'd love to, Derek, but I really need to crash now. How about we discuss it over breakfast, or lunch, or whatever meal they're serving in the cafeteria when I finally wake up. Deal?" he asked.

"Deal! I need to crash too." He got up and stretched, yawning out the next bit, "Oh, and remind me to kick your ass when we're feeling up to it. I have forgiven you yet."

"Duly noted. See you in a few hours," called out Alistair before falling face first, fully clothed onto his bed.

CHAPTER

FORTY-ONE

AFTER THE MEMORIAL, everyone went to the cafeteria for a light lunch. Classes were canceled that afternoon and some students were already leaving for the weekend.

Tom sat with Benny, Zaina, and Arturo. He picked at his food; they all did.

"Where do you think they took her?" asked Benny.

He meant Mandy, of course. The last they'd seen her, she'd been frozen but alive.

"I heard they placed her in a vacuum chamber and took her to The Hold," said Arturo.

Tom was surprised. Until he'd visited the Honeywells, he had no idea what was going on.

"How can you possibly know that?" asked Zaina.

"I heard the other den mothers talking about it. Masha, the DM for year five, has an uncle who works there," he said.

"Is it true?" Zaina asked, this time addressing Tom.

Tom nodded. "I went to see her parents yesterday," replied Tom.

"Really? How did they react?" asked Zaina.

"They were really decent. I was expecting them to ask me to take her place or something. Which I was prepared to do, but it wouldn't bring her back at this point."

Everyone nodded.

"So, if my sci-fi knowledge is to be trusted, by placing her into a vacuum chamber, they've basically killed her in an airtight container," Benny ventured.

Zaina gasped. "That's terrible! You mean it's like going into space without a spacesuit?"

"Pretty much, but it's not as dramatic as you make it out to be. First, she was already frozen, and her vitals were low. Second, once you remove the air from a chamber, it takes less than thirty seconds for someone to lose consciousness, and they die in under two minutes. Since Mandy was already unconscious, she probably died in under sixty seconds," replied Arturo.

Zaina shuddered and Benny took deep calming breaths and fanned his eyes to avoid crying.

"From what the Honeywells told me, an extraction team came to pick her up. They placed her in the chamber and supplied her with oxygen during transport. Miss Clementine and Lady Mathilda were there the whole time and told Mrs. Honeywell that Mandy looked like Snow White in her glass coffin.

Lady Mathilda escorted Mandy to The Hold and stayed until the chamber was placed in a secure room. A canister was attached to the chamber to collect the air, and any other particles, or spirits, that would be removed from the chamber in the vacuum sealing process."

"What did they do with Mandy's body?" asked Benny.

"What did they do with the canister?" asked Zaina.

"Mandy was cremated per her parents' wishes to ensure that she didn't have a body to jump back into if things went south. As for the canister, they've placed it in a lead-lined box inside an iron vault until they can figure out how to destroy it."

"How can we be sure it worked?" asked Benny.

"Yeah. How do we know for sure that someone didn't breathe it in?" said Arturo.

Tom thought about this.

"I was in the room with her when it happened, and I'd know if Brön had body-snatched me. I think it would be obvious to everyone who knows me," he said.

"Lady Mathilda brought her here. If any of you had breathed it in, you'd be dead or crazy powerful by now. The same goes for the teachers. I'm not sure about High Elves, but I'm pretty sure they are immune to possession."

Zaina was nodding. "Right, but what about the team that came to get her?"

"Lady Mathilda stayed with Mandy the whole time. If the spirit had gotten out between the vacuum and vaulting processes, surely there would be dead bodies lying about. I don't think it can survive without a body. And for now, I don't think it can escape its container."

"So, it's over?" asked Benny.

"Yeah, I'd say it's over," replied Tom.

CHAPTER
FORTY-TWO

TOM WANTED to do something nice for his friends, and he also wanted to distract himself until he could see Lola. She'd be in classes all day and would probably have dinner with her family when she got home. By the time she would be done, it would be too late in the UK to go over.

He'd sent her a Traveling letter last night and they agreed to spend the day together on Saturday. Since his travel ban was now lifted, he told her to wear comfortable shoes and bring her passport.

"What are you doing this afternoon?" he asked Zaina, Arturo, and Benny. The cafeteria was emptying, yet they'd made no move to leave.

All of them answered some variation of going home and chilling out.

"Want to take a trip? I promise to have you home by dinner time, or whenever you need to be home," Tom said, rubbing his hands in anticipation.

"Are you allowed to be taking us all over the world?" asked Benny.

"That's an excellent question, Benny! I did, in fact, check The Traveler's Handbook. It clearly states that I cannot expose my Key, Door, or other Traveling accouterments to humans, aka spells and such. Nowhere does it say that I cannot share my ability with Witches and

Warlocks," he exclaimed. To emphasize his point, he pulled the Handbook from his pocket. He'd used the spell to miniaturize it and had vowed to always carry it from now on.

Zaina laughed and said, "Put your book of baby spells away. I was in the minute you said trip!"

"Me too!" replied Arturo.

"Well, I'm not staying behind! Where shall we go?"

They debated it for a while but decided to go back to Zaina's house in Lebanon. It was warm, sunny, and there was sure to be food.

"Get your stuff and let's meet out front in thirty minutes. Is that enough time?" Tom asked.

They all but ran out of the room, pushing each other to get through the door. Tom was happy they were excited about the trip. It had been a while since he'd been excited about much of anything. As for Traveling, he'd always taken it for granted, especially as all his friends could do it too.

Now that he was among non-Travelers, it made him feel special and he realized how cool it was to have a magic Key that could open a Door to anywhere in the world.

Tom packed his bag and gave his mom a call to let her know he'd be home soon, but only to drop off his bag and grab his cell phone before he went out again with his friends.

He answered all her questions and was relieved to know she wouldn't be home. She was having tea in Milan with a friend before heading to some art exhibit. She wouldn't be home until late, but she was very glad he had called.

When he got outside, he saw his friends were already there. He asked if they were okay with him dropping his bag off at his house and grabbing his phone and swimsuit.

"I'd love to see where you live!" exclaimed Zaina.

"Would it be too much trouble to stop by my place and do the same? I couldn't reach my parents, so this way I could leave a note and they won't worry," said Benny.

"I don't mind if the others don't," replied Tom.

"I don't mind. Especially if we can drop by my place too!" said Arturo, for once unsure of himself.

"It's fine with me. Just remember that it's four hours later in Sidon, so we'll get there around five after all our pit stops. That should make the sun and heat more tolerable anyway. Count me in!"

"I've never been to anyone's house that I met at school. This is beyond cool!" said Benny.

Tom took out his Key and opened a Door to his house first. He gave his friends a quick tour, pointing out the suit of armor and making sure to visit the study. Inquiring minds wanted to know! They took a minute of silence in the study in honor of Mandy's sacrifice before continuing their house-hopping tour.

Next up was Benny's home in Richmond. When Benny was showing them around the stately home, Tom couldn't help thinking his mom would love the antiques and the impressionist art hanging on the walls.

They didn't linger and quickly moved on to Arturo's home in Palermo, Italy. He lived with his deaf grandmother in a three-room walk-up in a more rural part of town. Mercifully, his grandmother was out that afternoon and they didn't have to sit, eat cake, and explain how they had traveled here. *Nonna* wasn't a Witch, and the explanation would have been lengthy.

They made it to Zaina's house a little after five. Zaina had called ahead, and the ladies fussed over Benny. Once they'd eaten a snack, they were shooed from the kitchen to go play outside like children.

The boys stayed until after one a.m., which was only nine p.m. on UK time. But they'd had fun and looked forward to doing it again soon.

Tom dropped the guys off and went home to an empty house. Tabitha had come and gone. She was spending the weekend at her new boyfriend's house in Ibiza or some other trending hot spot.

Tom was happy to have the place to himself. He took a shower and put on his favorite pajamas. He could have gone down to their TV room, but it felt cozier to just stay in his room. He grabbed his laptop and settled in bed to binge-watch all the shows he'd missed in the last few weeks.

It had started out as a horrible day. But spending time with his friends and goofing off had reminded him that life did go on, even after the most traumatic events. People still had to eat, sleep, and try to find joy where they could.

It was good to be home.

CHAPTER

FORTY-THREE

TOM SHOWED up at Lola's house at nine a.m. the next day. He was thrilled that Lola had agreed to get an early start because it was already two p.m. for him, and he didn't think he could wait any longer than that.

They were expecting him for breakfast. Lola and Devlin's aunt and uncle wanted to hear Tom's story too, so he would get that out of the way.

"Will you be staying on at Harding or returning to The Academy?" asked Phyllis.

Tom looked at Lola. They hadn't had a chance to discuss it yet.

"I thought I might finish the semester and take it from there. With everything that's gone on, I can't say I've given Harding all that much of a chance. What little classes I've had were interesting and useful. I haven't discussed it with the Headmistress yet, but perhaps I might forgo the full magical curriculum they had initially set out for me since I don't have any special magical gifts. That way, I could focus on my Uni classes since I'm already behind as it is," he replied.

"No silly, you're not behind, remember? You and I are a year early due to Custodian Duties, which I no longer have," said Lola.

"Indeed," said Devlin, "Isn't attending The Academy mandatory for all Custodians?

Tom's face went blank. "You're right, it is! I can't believe I forgot that."

Boris got up and started clearing the table. "That's understandable. I'm sure Headmaster Lianon will allow you to finish your semester at Harding. If you really wanted to pursue your education there in the fall, surely an agreement could be made. Perhaps summer classes?"

Lola and Tom groaned in unison.

"What did I say?" asked Boris before leaving for the kitchen.

"That would be just our luck. Me attending Harding with summer classes at The Academy while Lola attends The Academy with summer classes at Harding," explained Tom.

"Oh. I see your point!" said Boris on his way out.

"I'm sure you kids will figure it out. So long as everyone is in school, I'm certain the adults will be amenable to any solution," put in Phyllis as she rose from the table.

"If you'll excuse me, I must see to the twins. We've just hired a new nanny and I like to check up on her periodically," explained Phyllis.

"Thank you for breakfast, Phyllis," said Tom, rising.

"You're welcome, sugar. I hope to see you soon," she replied, and turned to Lola, "Have fun on your outing!"

After she'd gone, they left the dining room and headed for the foyer. Devlin asked where they were going.

"It's a surprise," Lola answered, clapping her hands in excitement.

"May I have a word, Tom, before you go?" asked Devlin.

"Yeah, sure," replied Tom. He winked at Lola as he followed Devlin to his study.

It was weird having a study at their age. Although Devlin was over eighteen, and regularly reminded Lola and Tom that he was an adult, he still looked like a kid behind his father's desk.

"I'd like to know where you are taking my sister, what you plan on doing there, and when you will be returning," he said, hands clasped in front of him, straight-faced, like he was conducting an important business deal.

Tom knew the drill and he admired Devlin's protective nature.

"I'm taking Lola to Paris to make up for our botched date. We'll start at Notre Dame, visit the old chapel, walk to the Louvre, explore the museum for a few hours, then stroll through the Tuileries Garden and finish with dinner on the Bateau-Mouche. If there's time, we might explore the Latin quarter. Does that meet with Monsieur's approval?" quipped Tom.

"Yes, that is an acceptable itinerary. You will have your phone on you?" he asked.

"Of course. As will Lola, who also has a Key and could leave any time she wanted," Tom said.

"Yes, I will remind her of that before you go. Very well, you have my blessing," replied Devlin.

Tom tried not to laugh. Their relationship was still on the mend, and he didn't want to antagonize his friend. While Tom was now devoid of magical abilities, Devlin still had his.

He could totally kick Tom's butt if he wanted to.

"I'll keep her safe, I promise," said Tom in all sincerity.

"And happy?" asked Devlin.

"And happy."

CHAPTER
FORTY-FOUR

TOM HAD WANTED to arrive near a landmark Lola would immediately recognize. However, as he'd never been to Paris on his own, he didn't know the best spots to arrive by Door. Once Devlin had concluded his older brother talk, he had suggested a few alterations to Tom's itinerary that would enable a more discreet arrival and departure.

They arrived at the Luxembourg Gardens, in the path behind the *Orangerie*. Devlin had been right. It was deserted.

They followed the path back to the main thoroughfare that led directly to the front of Luxembourg Palace. Lola clapped in excitement and asked if there was time for a visit.

"That depends on how much time you think you might need at the Louvre," replied Tom.

Lola bit her lip and frowned with such concentration, that Tom laughed and said, "You know we can come back anytime, right?"

She relaxed and placed a hand on Tom's forearm. "Of course. Let's do the quick tour and come back to visit the places we like best," she said sensibly.

Tom placed his hand over hers. He liked the feeling of her fingers absently brushing the hairs on his arm. He felt the heat of her hand on his skin radiate all over his body and tore his gaze away from their hands to meet her eyes.

Lola searched his face for something. Was she checking to make sure he was Tom? *Her* Tom. The one she'd met at The Academy less than a year ago when he was still an innocent kid of fifteen and her fresh from her sweet-sixteen ball in Virginia.

He let her look and didn't speak. Instead, he turned to face her completely, placing his feet so the tips of their shoes touched, and took both her hands.

Her gaze was like a caress. It started with the top of his head, taking in his dark hair, almost reaching his shoulders now, as he hadn't had a haircut in ages. The good news was that he was able to tuck the strand of hair that always fell in his eyes behind his ear.

Next, she examined his forehead, her eyes trailing down along his jaw, lingering on his mouth and sweeping back up to meet his eyes. He held her gaze, opening up as much as he could so that she could see his very soul.

He tried to convey how sorry he was for everything that had happened, for causing her even the briefest moment of worry or doubt, for not living up to her expectations, and for not treating her with the respect and devotion she deserved.

It should have been awkward, staring into each other's eyes for so long, oblivious to the passersby as they stood in front of the Palace. It wasn't. It felt exactly right. As Tom bore into Lola's soul, he felt her acknowledge his apology and absolved him of his guilt.

He smiled. She smiled. His eyes strayed to her mouth, which parted slightly, ready for the kiss they hadn't shared in weeks but had lingered between them like an ache. He bent down and lightly touched her lips with his. She sighed, relaxing her shoulders, and leaning toward him like she was being pulled by an unseen gravitational force.

Tom felt himself relax as well, his body loose, but oddly grounded to the earth for the first time in weeks, maybe months. Like he and Lola were rooted to the spot where they stood and nothing could dislodge them, not even a hurricane.

He released her hands and placed his own on either side of her head to deepen the kiss. She opened up for him, their tongues meeting, dancing, lingering. They kissed and they kissed, Her arms wrapped around him, pulling him closer until his foot had to slip between hers to maintain his equilibrium.

He ran his hands through her hair, massaging her scalp, and still, they kissed. She ran hers up and down his back, urging him closer as she kneaded the muscles of his lower back.

I never want to stop. I could kiss this girl forever.

He held her close to him until not even a feather could have fit between them.

Same.

Tom blinked his eyes open but didn't release Lola's lips.

Did you just answer me? he thought.

Yeah, I guess I did, replied Lola inside his head.

He broke away from her lips and cupped her face with his hands.

"Did we just communicate telepathically?" he asked.

"Yup," she replied and was leaning in to resume kissing when they were interrupted by applause and French exclamations of "*Ah, l'amour!*"

They broke apart and took in their surroundings. Not three feet away from them, a mime was kissing the air, arms wrapped around his imaginary partner.

Lola's hands flew to her flushed cheeks, and she shook her head in mortification. Tom's face was also flaming, and he took Lola's hand to tug her away from the spectacle. The mime followed them as he roused the crowd to applaud for another round of applause.

Tom and Lola waited for the gathered people to let them pass. The audience wasn't quite done with them, so Tom turned and waved at them with his free hand and said, "*Merci beaucoup! J'adore cette fille!*"

He wrapped an arm around Lola's waist, dipped her, and planted a theatrical kiss on her lips before pulling her back up. It wasn't as easy as it appeared in the movies, but no one seemed to mind his amateurish delivery because the crowd roared with applause. Red-faced and breathless, Tom and Lola took their bow and made a run for it.

MARIE-HÉLÈNE LEBEAULT

They ran down the path away from the Palace, past the fountain, all the way to the actual garden where they paused to catch their breaths. They got a drink from a street vendor and sat on the chairs around the garden.

Did you mean it? asked Lola with her mind.

What? asked Tom.

What you said before you dipped me, she said.

That I adore you? Absolutely! replied Tom.

He got up and held out his hand to her.

She smiled up at him, took his hand, and let him pull her up and into one of his legendary bear hugs.

They stayed there for a minute and when they broke apart Lola yelled, "*J'adore ce garçon!*" before planting a smacking kiss on Tom's lips. They burst out laughing but got no applause this time.

"Shall we continue our tour?" asked Tom.

"Lets. Where to next?" she asked.

"I was thinking of a visit to the Pantheon," he said.

"Excellent suggestion!" she replied, and they strolled arm and arm.

On the ten-minute walk to the famous landmark, they discussed Tom's sudden ability to communicate telepathically.

"Do you think my powers are coming in like yours?" he asked.

"I don't know. When we tested them back at The Academy, you didn't seem to have the same abilities as Devlin and me," she replied.

"Do you think it was the ring? It might have interfered with the process. You got yours when you met Devlin right? How long after your birthday was that? Do think it has any bearing?"

There were so many questions What if it was a fluke.

Can you still hear me? he asked anxiously.

Yes, Tom. Don't worry. That's my job, remember? she replied.

"Okay. Maybe tomorrow we could do some more testing. That is if you're not sick of me by the end of the day," he said.

"I won't be sick of you," she said. They had arrived at their destination and took some time to visit and take pictures, which they shared with their friends on the private group Snapchat they had created.

They headed to the Notre Dame Cathedral next. Lola was obsessed with the gargoyles, so they tracked up the stairs to get a closer look. She pointed out the actual gargoyles, and the other the chimera: the wyvern, the striga, and the grotesques, explaining the subtle differences between them.

"Chimera are purely ornamental. While they serve a protection purpose, they don't have the same functional purpose that gargoyles have, which is to carry rainwater away from the building."

Once she'd had her fill with monsters, they headed to the Louvre to satisfy her other artistic cravings. She oohed and ahhed at everything like the American tourist that she was. In anyone else, the level of enthusiasm would have been annoying. But as this was Lola, and it was adorable.

They spent an hour below stairs with the Italian statues. Lola's hands hovered as close to the figures as she dared.

"I could spend hours on this floor alone!" she said when Tom announced the museum would be closing soon.

"We can come back as often as you like. Every weekend if we have to!" he replied, and she giggled.

"Do you want to have a quick peek at the Mona Lisa before we go?"

"OMG! Yes! How can I come to the Louvre and not see the Mona Lisa!" she exclaimed as she pulled him toward the elevator.

"Don't get too excited. It's behind protective glass and often surrounded by a lot of people," he warned. He hated to burst her bubble, but it was better to adjust her expectations.

"Oh, right. Of course," she said, her excitement only slightly dimmed.

The crowd was manageable, and they were able to observe the grand lady from as many angles as it took to get a view that didn't include a reflection. Lola was satisfied and they left the museum.

They walked along the Seine, through the Tuileries Garden until they reached the Place de la Concorde. They strolled around for an hour, taking in the sights until it was time to board the Bateau-Mouche for dinner. They walked along the Seine to the port where the river cruise departed.

When they arrived, Lola expressed concerns about her attire upon seeing the beautiful ship. Tom pointed out the people who were boarding ahead of them. Most people were tourists dressed as casually as they were.

It was a two-hour cruise with a four-course dinner. It felt good to be sitting down after so much walking. The cruise took them past the Louvre, Notre Dame Cathedral, and the Eiffel Tower, illuminated now that night had fallen.

They were served wine with their meal though they hadn't asked for it, nor expected it.

"I don't think either of us looks old enough to pass for eighteen," Lola said.

"The French don't consider wine with a meal to be underage drinking per se. Besides, how many teenagers do you see on the boat?" Tom asked.

Lola looked around at the diners. Most were couples talking softly, holding hands, and reveling in each other's company.

When the first course arrived, Lola forgot about everyone, even the view. She was a total foodie, and Tom knew she was about to provide him with much better entertainment than the band that was playing behind them.

"Oh. My. God," exclaimed Lola as she tasted the duck liver paté they were served with a garnish of caramelized onions and a single truffle. "This is so good!"

Beyond Lola's vocal appreciation of the meal, they didn't speak much while they ate, content to listen to the music and soak in Paris in all its romantic splendor.

Over coffee and dessert, a pear and chocolate tart that had Lola in raptures to the point that Tom offered her his own just so he could bask in culinary joy, they discussed what they might do the next day, aside from testing Tom's powers.

"I don't ever want this night to end," said Tom as he sat back in his chair, his belly full and his heart bursting.

"Maybe it doesn't have to," replied Lola, meeting his eyes.

CHAPTER

FORTY-FIVE

THE SERVER CAME to clear the table and announced they would be arriving to port in fifteen minutes. It gave Tom a few minutes to process what Lola had just said. Had she said what he thought she said? Then, he wondered if she could read his thoughts and clammed up.

"What did you have in mind?" he asked, hoping he sounded casual.

Lola blushed, betraying her thoughts without having to speak them aloud or telepathically.

Tom's mouth went dry, and he cursed the waiter for removing their water glasses.

His voice cracked a little when he said, "My family has a flat in Paris."

Lola didn't break eye contact when she replied, "So does mine."

Tom's mouth had now filled with saliva as he imagined any number of scenarios where he and Lola were alone in a room, a bedroom, with neither chaperone nor interruption. He swallowed audibly and was about to ask some follow-up questions when he felt someone brush past him.

The ship had stopped, and half the diners had already left. It was Tom's turn to be red-cheeked as he ushered Lola off the boat. They held hands and did not speak as they made their way back to the walkway along the Seine. Since they hadn't decided which of the flats they would be visiting, or even if it was a wise course of action, Tom stopped when he spotted a free bench. They sat down.

"Our flat is near the Champs Élysées," he said, looking out at the water. They were still holding hands.

"Ours is near the Arc du Triomphe," she said.

"That's further and I wager Devlin knows where it is," Tom said.

"You may be right. If I don't come home by midnight, he may very well start looking for me. Even though Phyllis herself gave me the code to the keypad and suggested I might want to stay the night. I don't think she meant with you though," smirked Lola.

Tom thought they could easily head to the flat and spend most of the night together, set an alarm, and make it back to Virginia by midnight. It was ten forty-five in Paris, but only five forty-five back home.

When he explained his logic to her, Lola was delighted.

"What about you though?" she asked. "Won't you get into trouble? Won't you be tired?"

Tom chuckled and told her his mom was in Milan and wouldn't notice when he came home. It wasn't strictly the truth, but he wanted to put her at ease. He could deal with his mother's displeasure if it meant spending quality time alone with Lola.

Tom squeezed Lola's hand. "Are you ready?"

She squeezed it back and turned to look at him.

"Not for.... that," she said, and he saw her cheeks turn crimson under the lamplight. "But I'm ready to go if that's what you mean." She stared out at the water, rubbing her free hand on her jeans in a nervous gesture.

With his other hand, Tom placed a finger under her chin so she would face him again. He leaned in a placed a light kiss on her lips. "All I want to do is hold you, kiss you, and maybe watch the sun come up while holding your hand. Anything beyond that can wait until we're both ready."

CHAPTER
FORTY-SIX

THEY SAT on the roof at five-thirty the next morning, bundled up in blankets, hands wrapped around strong cups of coffee, waiting for the sun to come up. They sat hip-to-hip, moving in harmony as they shared a packet of stale biscuits and a can of peaches they'd found in the pantry.

Tom had texted his mom the night before to let her know he'd be staying over at a friend's house. She was so happy that he had checked in that she forgot to ask any follow-up questions. She was also slightly tipsy and that always helped. He suggested she stay the night in Milan and she thought that was a marvelous idea.

Lola had texted Phyllis to say she'd be coming home past midnight and wouldn't be staying at the Paris flat.

When Devlin texted at midnight asking why she wasn't home yet, she replied that she would come home when she was good and ready and that she was perfectly capable of protecting her own virtue, thank you very much.

Fortunately, their telepathic connection did not reach this far, and she didn't have to listen to a lecture on boys' intentions.

She laughed when he followed up with a text to Tom that read:

`Touch her and you die.`

Tom did not laugh and sent back the only reply he could.

`Duly noted.`

Then they both laughed and tossed their phones to focus on the rising sun.

Once they'd finished their snack, they tidied up and said goodnight. The plan was to get some sleep in their respective beds and meet up at Lola's after breakfast.

"I THINK astral projection is going to take time to master," Lola said after Tom's third unsuccessful attempt.

"The good news is it's something they teach at Harding so I should maybe keep up with my magic classes," Tom replied.

The other good news is that you and Lola will have some distance during the week, thought Devlin.

Dude, nothing happened. I swear! replied Tom in his mind.

That experiment had been conclusive. Tom could communicate with Devlin as well, much to his chagrin. Devlin had been having a great time admonishing him in private thoughts directed only at Tom.

It had taken some practice, but they had managed to have a three-way conversion. The trick was to intentionally include both people when addressing them.

And while astral projection has been a bust, Tom had managed telekinesis, weak as it was.

He could move small objects a few inches, a far cry from being able to throw an entire bureau across the room, but it was a good start. Tom would practice and get better.

Inspired by Tom's new abilities, Phyllis asked to be tested next.

"If y'all have powers, I don't see why your daddy and I wouldn't have them too. If all that was standing in the way of your powers was a binding spell, I assume the spell was lifted for all Evers, not just for you," she told Lola, Devlin, and Tom after they'd had lunch.

Being a veteran meditator, she pickup up astral projection in no time, and was excited to communicate with the youngsters by telepathy. When she called a bottle to her and it came flying through the room, she said, "Oh this is going to come in so handy with the babies!"

Boris, who'd just walked in the front door, asked, "What is going to be handy?"

"Check this out, sugar," drawled Phyllis as she took an apple from the fruit basket and sent it over to Boris with your mind.

Boris looked at the apple float through the air between them and reached out to grasp it when it was within reach. "That's extraordinary! How did you do that?" he asked in his thick Russian accent, still marveling at the apple he held in his hand.

"I'll tell you later," she said with a wink.

"Yes, yes," he replied absently as he walked over to kiss her cheek and put the apple back in the basket.

"Do you think the twins can do this too?" he asked.

Phyllis blanched and her hand flew to her mouth. "Son of a nutcracker! I hadn't thought of that!"

She struggled out of her chair and fled the room, pausing briefly at the door to tell the kids to have a lovely afternoon, the embodiment of southern hospitality.

"Boris?" she called out.

"Coming, my sweet," he said and, with a bow, left the kids to clear the tables as he rushed after his frantic wife.

They cleared the dishes and filled the dishwasher. Devlin excused himself saying he was meeting Sara, his girlfriend, for a few hours before it was time to go back to school.

Lola walked Tom out. He needed to be back at Harding by six p.m. if he didn't want to miss dinner, which was ridiculous because he'd just had lunch. They laughed at the idiosyncrasies of the magical life and made out a little before he really had to go.

Their experience in Paris had cured them both of their aversion to PDA and they were willing to make out anywhere, anytime they could get their hands on each other.

Devlin had been right though. Being in separate schools would provide some much-needed distance. Painful as it might be to be away from Lola all week, Tom knew they would both do better in their classes if they weren't joined at the hip, or rather, the lips.

Early in their relationship, they'd had to cram a year's worth of classes in four months so they could start Uni in the Winter semester. As it was their first real relationship, spending time together studying and keeping things PG-14 had been enough for them.

Then, they'd been too busy with all the craziness to give it much thought. Or, if they had been thinking of taking things to the next level, they certainly hadn't had the opportunity.

Things were different now. They unleashed the beast, so to speak. The veil of innocence had been lifted, and it was a matter of time before their love story became R-rated.

On that thought, Tom gave Lola's butt a squeeze before he let her go, gauging her reaction.

"Don't you be starting something we can't finish, Tom Callahan," she said, hands on hips, but tongue-in-cheek.

"I love it when you talk dirty to me," he replied, and she burst out laughing. He gave her another mind-blowing kiss and pulled out his Key.

"Save that thought until next week," he said as he waved at her from his bedroom in Cork. When she made to follow him, he blew her a kiss and closed the door.

The last thing he heard was Lola calling him a tease and he chuckled to himself.

CHAPTER
FORTY-SEVEN

THE SEMESTER FLEW BY, and Tom couldn't believe how well things were going with Lola.

He'd spent the last few months dividing his time between his old friends and his new friends.

Though he and Lola spent as much time alone as they could, they also didn't want to turn into the kind of couple that ignored their friends.

Every weekend, they balanced their time between family, each other, and their friends.

There was always a party or a get-together somewhere, hosted either by their Traveler friends or by Tom's new Harding friends.

Arturo, Zaina, and Benny had taken to Lola immediately, but the jury was still out on Devlin. He was just too laced up and uptight for them. However, once Benny and Devlin discovered that they were both movie and art fiends, a new friendship was born.

A week or so before finals, Tom received an unexpected visitor at Harding Academy. He went down to the visitor's lounge to find Alistair waiting for him.

They grabbed a beverage and sat down.

"First, I'd like to apologize for how things went down when we first met. I was sorry to have deceived you because I thought we'd have gotten along well if it hadn't been for this evil Master business," Alistair began.

"Fair enough," replied Tom. He wasn't about to tell this guy that he'd looked forward to being mentored by someone he'd immediately looked up to.

"I thought you might be interested in an update on the situation. I'm not supposed to share the details of the investigation outside the MFO or the CEMB, but I think you deserve the truth and I'm sure I can count on your discretion," he said.

"I appreciate that and, yes, I promise I won't say a word," replied Tom.

"As you know, The Master turned out to be Brendan Callahan, your grandfather. Before he faked his own death, his Will named your father as his heir, and he inherited all the properties and assets listed in it.

When Brendan inherited from our great grandfather, he kept the family home and most of the assets but gave Brian, his twin, and my grandfather, a smaller Estate, and a generous amount of money. He also set aside a generous dowry for their sister, whom you should know is Jameson's grandmother," said Alistair. He paused to let Tom absorb this news.

"Are you talking about the Jameson I think you're talking about?" asked Tom as he mimed a mangled face.

Alistair nodded.

"Yes, we are all second cousins."

"Did he know that when he attacked me last February?" asked Tom.

Alistair shrugged. "It's hard to say. What I know is that Brendan/Brön left control of his company to the three of us."

"What? That's crazy, we're just kids. No offense, but you're what, twenty-two? And Jameson can't be older than eighteen," Tom said.

"None taken. And you're right about our ages. Since I'm the only one of us who's over twenty-one and have been acting DG for the past three months, and the fact that I've done a good job at it, the Board has elected me as DG. I have accepted the position."

"So, you're running everything now? What about your job at the MFO?" asked Tom.

"I'm not running everything. The CEO takes care of the day-to-day operations. As Director General, I represent the owners, the Board, and the shareholders and ensure the CEO follows our guidelines. As far as my job at the MFO, I was quite bored with it before I took this mission. However, now that I've had a taste for 'active' fieldwork, I must admit it requires a level of fortitude I may not possess. Also, I've met someone," said Alistair, a shy smile appearing on his lips.

"That's great. Is it someone at the company?" asked Tom.

"Yes, he's part of the HR team. When I was hired, there were tasks where I interacted with an anonymous person. When we were finally introduced, he told me I had an exceptional mind. I'm a sucker for compliments," he said, blushing a little.

"That's awesome. I'm happy for you. I can imagine being a secret agent was lonely work," replied Tom.

"Yeah, it was. Anyhow, the Board has stipulations and would like to meet you and Jameson at your earliest convenience.

"Stipulations?" asked Tom.

"They'll go over each of them with you at the meeting, but essentially, they refuse to sign cheques to someone they've never met. Also, they expect you to attend at least three annual Board meetings and participate in a summer internship the year you graduate from University," he said.

Tom said nothing for a beat. Then, he scratched his head and frowned.

"Back up for a minute. When you say Brendan has left control of the company to the three of us. You mean, he wants us to run it together?" he asked.

"Technically yes, but we don't have to be involved beyond attending Board meetings. I just happen to like the work."

"And you said something about cashing cheques. You mean we'll get paid whether we work there or not?" Tom asked.

"Yes, provided you've made an effort to learn about the company and involve yourself in the decisions during the Board meetings, you will receive your share of the profits."

"A third?"

"Not exactly. We three own fifty-one percent of the company. The board owns forty percent, and the rest is publicly owned by share-holders."

Tom nodded.

"Ok, and the internship. Is that in the hopes that we work there?"

"Yes and no. You could if you wanted to, and you'd be paid a hand-some salary if you were hired, but ultimately, it's for you to get a working knowledge of what we do there," replied Alistair.

"And what do we do there, exactly?" asked Tom.

"You'll have to attend a Board meeting for that," said Alistair, tongue-in-cheek.

"Ok, one more question."

"Shoot."

"Do I have to attend the same Board meeting as Jameson? I don't think I'm ready to see him just yet," replied Tom.

"No, you don't. And I totally get that. Now, onto the classified information."

Alistair went on to say that the investigation that had started with Phyllis Evers' kidnapping was finally closed. All guilty parties had been arrested, including Jameson and his father, the two missing conspirators in the artifact thefts. The CEMB had been lenient with Jameson due to his age, and he'd been sent to a magical reform school in Alaska to finish his degree in finance. His father was serving time at The Hold.

"I guess I won't be running into my new cousin anytime soon," said Tom.

"No, rest assured. You will also be happy that you will not see an accidental resurgence of Brön the Witch Hunter. His tube left The Hold last week with one of your Academy teachers, Professor Thunderbolt. Headmaster Lianon opened a Portal so he could take it off-planet and ensure no human would ever host this specific brand of evil ever again."

"That's good to know."

Alistair rummaged through his pocket and pulled out a small black felt bag, which he handed to Tom.

"What is it?"

"Open it."

Tom undid the strings and turned the bag upside down over his hand. A red stone slid out. He sent a questioning look to Alistair.

"It's the garnet from your father's ring. I thought you might want it. The stone didn't melt with the ring."

Tom immediately dropped the stone on the floor and stepped away from it.

Alistair put up a hand to reassure him. "Don't worry, it's been examined by no less than fifty specialists, both human and magical. It's just a pretty rock now," he said as he picked up the stone and put it back in the felt bag.

"I don't want it," said Tom, looking warily at Alistair's outstretched hand.

"You don't have to carry it. Maybe you could put it in your vault at home. You could even sell it," he suggested.

Tom took the bag and held it gingerly by the strings. He would give the bag to Headmaster Lianon when next he saw him and ask him to put it someplace safe.

"Anyhow, now that I'm no longer in the spy business, I thought it might be nice to get a life. Would you be interested in getting together at some point over the Summer?" asked Alistair. He sounded awkward, and unsure if the olive branch would be accepted.

"Do you enjoy hiking by any chance?" asked Tom.

Alistair's face lit up, "Why, yes. How did you know?"

"I didn't. I'd like to hike a mountain in America, and I've never been hiking. Might be a good idea to have an expert tag along," Tom said as nonchalantly as he could.

Alistair tried to remain aloof, but he was unsuccessful. I would love to go hiking with you, Tom. But surely there are more than enough mountains in the UK and Europe to keep us busy many an outing."

When Tom explained it was to honor Mandy's memory, Alistair had agreed on the spot.

Hopefully, it would be the first of many adventures the cousins would share.

CHAPTER

FORTY-EIGHT

IN JULY, while Lola and Devlin had their two-week magic classes at Harding, Tom spent those two weeks at The Academy learning about the ins and outs of Custodianship.

They had agreed to wait until after their Summer classes to decide what to do about school.

Tom now saw the benefit of pursuing his education at Harding and he was hoping that Lola and Devlin would come to the same conclusion. The difficulty, for them, was that their father worked at The Academy and that's the only place they could spend time with him, due to his condition. Also, as an Art Major, Devlin got to spend even more time with his dad since he was one of the art teachers there.

Now that he'd seen that they could make it work, even if they didn't attend the same university, Tom wasn't worried. He wanted Lola to make the best decision for herself and he knew that she was mature enough not to be swayed by his attempts at persuasion.

Meanwhile, Tom had requested an audience with Headmaster Lianon. His goal was to get the High Elf to invite him to the Summer Isles to test his powers. Now that even Phyllis Evers had powers, and they had ruled out Blood Magick as the source of Tom's new abilities, he was hoping the Headmaster would reconsider.

Tom almost choked on his tea when Lianon not only agreed but got up, pointed to his Portal window, and suggested they leave at once.

"Now?" asked Tom.

"Yes. Once your abilities have been tested and, hopefully, amplified, I thought you might help me with a thorny matter," said the Headmaster.

Proud as he was that the Headmaster might need his help with something, Tom couldn't imagine what it might be.

"Me, Sir? How could I help?"

"Remember Professor Thunderbolt?" asked the Headmaster.

Immediately, Tom got a sinking feeling in the pit of his stomach.

"Yes..."

"He left on an errand to his home planet a few weeks ago, but he hasn't returned. I'm worried about him. "

"Is that where he took the canister with The Master's...uh... remains?" asked Tom, bile rising in his throat.

"How would you know about that?" asked Lianon.

"I'm not at liberty to say, and I would appreciate it if you didn't probe my mind to find out Sir," replied Tom.

The Headmaster was surprised by Tom's request but honored it, nonetheless.

"Yes, that's where he took the... ah... canister."

"I see," said Tom, though he still didn't understand.

"I'm afraid there's more, Tom."

Tom knew even before the Headmaster said it. He looked toward the painting over the fireplace where the Headmaster's safe was located.

"Someone's taken the garnet. Am I right?"

"I would make a joke that your divination powers have improved, but I'm afraid it's no laughing matter."

Tom didn't reply. As awful as it made him feel to imagine Brön loose on another planet, it still felt like a win to him.

"Shouldn't we be hoping Professor Thunderbolt doesn't come back, Sir?" he said.

"Indeed, however, as the stone was taken weeks after Professor

Thunderbolt left, I'm not quite ready to connect the two incidents together. Especially as the thief took another object I would prefer to be returned to me as soon as possible," explained Lianon.

"You want me to retrieve this object? To find Professor Thunderbolt and ensure he's all right? Why can't you go yourself?" asked Tom, impatient for answers now.

"Yes, yes, and because my kind is no longer welcome on Lantil," he said slowly.

"Your *kind*, Sir?"

"People who can enter their planet without invitation."

Tom rubbed his forehead in confusion.

"What was the object that was taken from your safe, Sir?" asked Tom, trying to make sense of it all.

"It was Devlin's World Jumping Sphere. He gave it to me for safe-keeping before heading to Harding for his summer classes."

Tom thought that didn't sound like something Devlin would do, but he would circle back to that later.

"So, you think whoever took it used it to get to Lantil?" asked Tom.

"I don't think so, I *know* so. We can track Spheres from the Summer Isles. Whoever took it is still there," the High Elf said.

"And how does one receive an invitation to Lantil?" asked Tom.

"Tom, did Lola and Devlin tell you about their time at the Summers Iles?" asked Lianon with what looked like forced patience.

He nodded.

"Then you'll know that as soon as you arrive, with a simple touch I'll be able to answer all your questions and you'll have access to all the knowledge you've ever dreamed of. Now, do you need to call your mother before we go? I can have Lady Samsara take care of it for you," he said, edging his way to the Portal window in the corner of his office.

"Sure, I guess we can go then," said Tom as he followed the High Elf to the Portal. He paused at the other window, the one overlooking the grounds of The Academy. He felt the pull of the school and its Headmaster who'd always been there for him.

He felt torn once again between allegiances until he realized he didn't have to choose. He was a part of both the Traveling and Wizarding community. He didn't have to choose, he could combine.

It all made sense now. Studying international relations was about building bridges between communities and leveraging their combined strengths. High Elves didn't interfere with human lives, whether magical or not. But Tom could, he could at least try to make the world a better place for everyone. Not through domination, but through diplomacy.

Lola, Lianon is finally taking me to the Summer Iles! he thought.

Cool, when will you go?

Now! And I don't know when I'll be back.

Oh, ok... Have fun then and say hi to Aeriearie for me.

Will do. J'adore cette fille!

J'adore ce garçon!

Headmaster Lianon cleared his throat and Tom was startled.

"Shall we?" he asked, pointing to the swirling shimmer beyond which a whole new world beckoned.

Tom grinned. "Right behind you, Sir."

THE END

If you enjoyed this book, please consider leaving a review on Amazon, Goodreads, or Bookbub?

Reviews help me reach new readers and improve my craft.

Read **The Ancestors' Key**, the first book in **The Evers Series!**

www.ingramcontent.com/pod-product-compliance
Lightning Source LLC
Chambersburg PA
CBHW020327260626
47156CB00004B/1412